IN SEARCH OF LOVE

CONVENIENT ARRANGEMENTS (BOOK 2)

ROSE PEARSON

LANDON HILL MEDIA

IN SEARCH OF LOVE

Convenient Arrangements

(Book 2)

By

Rose Pearson

IN SEARCH OF LOVE

Miss Julianna Martins sighed heavily as she stepped into the ballroom. Even with her dear grandmother beside her, she felt her steps grow heavy as her reluctance grew.

"You must *try*, my dear girl."

"Yes, Grandmama," Julianna replied automatically, even though she knew that there was very little hope of her being noticed this evening, no matter what she did. She was plain, thin, and quiet, and with a father whom most of the *ton* despised, there was very little interest in her from any quarter. This was one of the first balls of the Season but Julianna felt no delight in such a thing. Rather, she wondered just how long she would have to remain before Lady Newfield would give up and allow her to return home.

"I know that your father has been less than helpful," Lady Newfield continued with a slight huff and a lift of her chin, "but I am here now and I fully intend to assist you this Season."

Julianna smiled slightly, looking across at Lady Newfield and feeling a small flicker of hope begin to burn in her heart.

It was quickly extinguished.

"You are very kind, Grandmama," she said honestly, looking back out across the ballroom and seeing that not a single pair of eyes had flicked in her direction as she continued to walk toward the left of the ballroom. "But everyone in the *beau monde* is well aware of who my father is and how little a dowry I have. Besides which, given that my father is a gambler, a drunkard, and very close to now being a pauper, I am quite certain that no sensible gentleman should want to come near to me!" She lifted one shoulder in a half-hearted shrug. "My father took great pleasure last Season to inform me that a gentleman spoke to him in the hope of courting me." Her heart began to ache as she recalled it. "He refused him. He stated that the gentleman did not have enough wealth in order to satisfy him. What he meant, of course, was that he was not a suitable gentleman for *him*. My father has long wanted me to wed a gentleman of great wealth and pliable character so that funds can be easily transferred to my father."

"All that is now at an end," Lady Newfield said firmly. "Your father has been spoken to and I have sworn to have you wed and settled by the time this Season is at an end."

Julianna did not know how to react to such a statement. She had long given up any expectation that the *ton* might show her even the smallest flicker of interest and certainly did not think that a gentleman of wealth, title, and good standing would even consider someone such as her. She knew precisely what she was to them. Nothing more than a wraith. A ghost that wandered through their midst without true form or any sort of worth.

Lady Newfield pursed her lips, her eyes narrowed and her gaze sharp. There was nothing said for a moment or two and Julianna knew that her grandmother was holding back all of the thoughts she would very much like to express about Viscount Fotheringhay, Julianna's father. Julianna knew very well that the match between her own late mother and Lord Fotheringhay had *not* been one blessed by Lady Newfield, but that she had not had the opportunity to voice such concerns. But it appeared that her concerns over Lord Fotheringhay had been quite correct. Ever since Julianna could remember, she had known her father to be arrogant, selfish, and entirely unconcerned about both herself and her mother. Not that Julianna could recall much about her dear mother, given that she had passed away from a great and terrible fever when Julianna had been but a few years old.

"Even if your father does not care about your future, Julianna, *I* do," Lady Newfield said eventually, each word forcible and determined. "I am all the more frustrated that he has kept me away from you these last few years."

Julianna gave her grandmother's arm a light squeeze. She knew all too well that the reason her father had kept Lady Newfield away from her was simply that he could not bear Lady Newfield's blunt manner and harsh words that flung the truth at him whenever she had cause to do so. They had met only on very brief occasions as Julianna had been growing up and yet, this year, Lady Newfield had not only written to inform Julianna's father that she would be in London to escort Julianna throughout society, but had also turned up at the door and walked straight through, without even a modicum of hesitation, and thereafter, had refused to depart without Julianna by her side.

Julianna was truly grateful to have her grandmother's company and wished she could find the words to express such a sentiment. Whilst she had no expectation that this evening's ball would be markedly different in any way from any previous balls, at least she now had someone by her side who truly cared about her.

"Your father, no doubt, left you to linger with the wallflowers at events such as these," Lady Newfield muttered darkly, as Julianna shot her a small, wry smile which betrayed the fact that this was precisely the truth. "Well, you can be assured, my dear Julianna, that *I* shall not be so unconcerned." She looked around the room a little more pointedly, her eyes assessing each and every face she saw. "We shall begin with introductions."

Julianna felt her stomach drop, the light smile falling away from her face almost at once. "Introductions?"

"Indeed," Lady Newfield said briskly. "I am certain that you know very few people here and I have no intention of allowing you to continue in such a small sphere."

She began to walk purposefully toward a group of ladies who were standing a little away from them, with Julianna noting how a few gentlemen were also making their way toward the group. Her stomach began to swirl in a most unwelcome manner, making her heart pound with trepidation. She wanted to pull her grandmother back, to inform her that she had no need to be introduced to anyone, given that they would do nothing other than bow or curtsy, exchange a few pleasantries, and then allow their gaze to drift away from her again, as she had seen so many times before.

But it was much too late. Before Julianna could protest, before she could even think to say that such an idea was not worth their while, Lady Newfield had tugged her into the group, curtsied, and then exclaimed so loudly that Julianna was certain that everyone in the room had heard it.

"Lady Tillsbury!" Lady Newfield cried, throwing her hands up in evident delight. "My goodness, I am so very glad to see you!"

There was a moment of silence and Julianna winced inwardly, certain that this would bring nothing but embarrassment to both herself and her grandmother, only for a second loud exclamation to rip through the ballroom as a lady seemingly acquainted with Lady Newfield tottered forward and threw her arms about her.

Julianna's mouth dropped open in surprise.

"I can hardly believe it!" Lady Tillsbury cried, holding onto Lady Newfield's upper arms and smiling broadly at her. "I did not think I should ever see you in London again!"

"It has been some years," Lady Newfield admitted, throwing a quick glance toward Julianna. "It has not been for lack of trying, I assure you, but you find me here at last."

Lady Tillsbury said something that Julianna could

not quite make out and Lady Newfield laughed gently, before turning to Julianna. Julianna, aware of Lady Tillsbury's immediate scrutiny, curtsied as gracefully as she could, feeling heat rise in her cheeks as she noted the others around them also showing her some interest. As she stood, she placed her hands gracefully in front of her but kept her head slightly bent, so that she would not be looking Lady Tillsbury directly in the face. It was not a matter of respect, however, but rather a habit that Julianna had become well used to, fearful that some sort of insult would be thrown at her, and thus she would be able to hide her expression rather well from such an angle.

It seemed Lady Tillsbury was not the sort of lady to insult others, however.

"I am *very* glad to meet the granddaughter of my dear friend," Lady Tillsbury said warmly, and Julianna looked up in surprise. The lady was smiling brightly, a sparkle in her eyes as she reached out to grasp Julianna's hands. "Tell me, have you long been in society?"

Julianna flushed. "Yes, my lady," she said, a little awkwardly. "This is now my third Season."

A small titter of laughter came from someone in the group and Julianna's color heightened all the more. Lady Tillsbury frowned at someone over Julianna's shoulder and immediately, the sound died away.

"Then I am all the more glad to make your acquaintance," she said firmly. "Allow me to introduce you to some of *my* acquaintances, who I am sure would be delighted to sign your dance card." This was said with what Julianna knew to be a pointed look at one or two others, and her blush continued filling her cheeks as she turned around to greet those Lady Tillsbury wished to introduce her to. She did her best to remain as dignified as she could, curtsying and greeting each person in turn with a quick smile, even though she could not bring herself to allow her eyes to linger on them for long.

It was not in vain that such introductions were made, however, for within a few minutes, Julianna found her dance card no longer entirely empty. Instead, she had three dances with three separate gentlemen, and although she knew that they were doing so simply to do as Lady Tillsbury asked, she could not help but feel a growing sense of delight deep within her. She was not going to be a wallflower this evening, it seemed!

"I thank you for your *kind* introductions, Lady Tillsbury," Lady Newfield said warmly. "If you will excuse me, I can see another dear friend that I simply must greet this evening."

Julianna smiled her thanks at Lady Tillsbury and took her leave, catching the victorious smile on her grandmother's face and unable to keep her own smile from growing steadily.

"You see?" Lady Newfield said triumphantly as she led Julianna through the crowd. "This evening shall not be as all your others have been, Julianna. I am quite determined that you will not hide in the shadows any longer!"

"You are very kind, Grandmama," Julianna answered truthfully, wishing she could express her sense of overwhelming gratitude to the lady and finding that flicker of hope beginning to burn again in her heart. This time, she did not immediately quench it but allowed it to burn, feeling it ignite her very soul. Her head lifted a little more, her shoulders straightened, and her chin held itself up a little higher. This evening, it seemed, the *ton* were going to take a little notice of her, whether they wished to or not.

Suddenly, quite out of nowhere, a long arm reached out and caught hers. With a gasp of astonishment, Julianna turned around to see a dark-haired gentleman with half-closed eyes, leering at her as he tugged her toward him.

She tried to call out but no sound left her mouth, such was her shock.

"There you are, Christina," the gentleman slurred, his other hand now holding her fast. "I have been looking all over the ballroom for you."

His eyes were dull, his smile sloping to one side of his face as he swayed heavily. Julianna's heart was beating furiously, her panic beginning to rise as she looked into the gentleman's face and tried her best to summon the strength to pull herself from him.

Unfortunately, even in his inebriated state, the gentleman's hands were much too tight. Julianna looked desperately for Lady Newfield, but her grandmother clearly thought that Julianna was still walking behind her and had not turned around to see that she was now absent.

"Please, sir," she said breathlessly, not wanting to speak too loudly for fear of drawing attention to herself. "I am not Christina."

The gentleman laughed and Julianna's face drained of color as he pulled her all the closer to him.

"You need not pretend," he said softly, one hand letting go of her arm so that he might trail his fingers down over her cheek. "I know that you have been longing for my attentions."

Julianna tried to pull herself free, shaking him off and turning on her heel as she did so, her breath quick and fast as she began to panic. She had to escape this cruel gentleman, to remove herself from him so that he would not make her shame and embarrassment all the greater— yet he would not allow her to depart.

His fingers grasped her arm firmly as she continued to try to wrench herself away, her eyes finally catching on Lady Newfield. Her grandmother was hurrying back toward her, her eyes wide with shock, clearly having realized that Julianna was no longer behind her as she made her way across the ballroom.

"Now, that is most unfair," the gentleman said, leaning down as Julianna pressed both hands against his chest to push herself from him. "You cannot truly wish to hide from me, not when I know what you have long been waiting for."

Before she could say anything, before she could raise a hand to slap him in an attempt to jolt him to his senses, the gentleman lowered his head and pressed his lips to Julianna's.

It was a horrifying moment. His lips were warm but damp, sliding across her lips until they lingered on her cheek. Julianna went limp, horror streaking through her as she realized what this now meant.

Gasps of shock came from all around her and, as she stepped back, the gentleman's fingers finally loosening on her arm, she saw the way those around her were whispering to each other, their hands at their mouths as they hid their remarks from her. The gentleman in question staggered to the right and then went crashing to the ground, bringing yet more shocked exclamations from those around him.

"Julianna!"

Lady Newfield was by her side, holding Julianna tightly as she stared, wide-eyed with shock, at the gentleman who now lay on the floor of the ballroom. "Whatever did he do?"

Julianna could barely find the energy to speak, such was her shock. Her fingers reached for Lady Newfield's hand, her whole body beginning to shake.

"He... he called me Christina," she whispered hoarsely. "I do not know who she is but he would not let me go."

Lady Newfield's eyes were flashing with fury but she maintained her composure with an effort. "It seems that he has tied you both together with his foolish actions," she said as people began to point at Julianna openly, without any sort of hesitation. "Forgive me, Julianna, but this must be done in order to preserve your reputation."

Julianna did not know what Lady Newfield meant, feeling the loss of her support keenly as Lady Newfield stepped forward, leaving Julianna to stand alone for a moment.

"I am very sorry that you have witnessed Lord Altringham behaving in such an inebriated and foolish manner," she said, addressing the crowd who now all watched Lady Newfield with great interest. "Evidently, he could not keep his admiration for Miss Julianna Martins, my granddaughter, to himself. I hope you will all join me in congratulating them both on their engagement."

Julianna felt the ground shift beneath her feet as she stared at her grandmother, seeing the grim smile that settled on the lady's face as she looked back at Julianna, a sharp look in her eye. Julianna tried to smile, her eyes filling with tears as Lady Newfield came back to her side, reaching out to hold her arm tightly as she did so.

"It will all be quite all right," Lady Newfield said firmly as the onlookers began to whisper and chatter to each other again, a new eagerness in their voices and demeanor. "You will see, my dear Julianna. It will all be quite all right."

CHAPTER ONE

"My *dear* Julianna."

Julianna tried to smile as her grandmother held her hands tightly in hers for a few moments, tears springing to her eyes as she looked into Lady Newfield's face and felt her heart tear apart.

"Are you quite ready?"

Julianna swallowed hard but nodded. "I suppose I must be, whether I wish to be present here or not."

The last few weeks had been something of a whirlwind. Lord Altringham had not come to see Julianna after he had awoken from his stupor, but rather had gone to her father to make the arrangements for the wedding. Julianna had been a little surprised that he had agreed to it without any sort of hesitation, but it seemed that Lord Altringham had been made fully aware of his actions and knew that he could not simply push aside such behavior as he had displayed the previous evening without consequence.

What had troubled her the most, however, was that

he had never once wished to greet her, to speak with her directly, or to even take tea with her! He had shown no interest in her whatsoever and had only communicated with her via notes. She had not remained in London but had returned to her father's estate almost at once, not wishing to remain in a society that would whisper about her without hesitation, yet she had found no solace in being back in her father's home.

Even now, as she stood on the threshold of the church, Julianna knew that she would be marrying a complete stranger who clearly had no consideration for her whatsoever.

The thought made her stomach twist with disappointment as tears blurred her vision. She ducked her head low.

"You must prepare yourself," Lady Newfield said firmly, pressing Julianna's hands. "What are your arrangements once the ceremony is at an end?"

Julianna shook her head, forcing her tears back. "I do not know," she said honestly. "Lord Altringham has not informed me of his intentions."

Lady Newfield's eyes flashed with the spark of anger that filled her at such words, her lips pulling thin.

"Then I shall remain with you, I think," she said decisively, making Julianna's heart leap with a sudden hope. "After all, it is quite common for a lady to take a relative with her on honeymoon, although I am aware it is not very often their grandmother that attends them!"

Julianna let out a small, broken laugh and embraced her grandmother, feeling as though her heart were breaking all over again. "I would be most grateful for your company, Grandmama," she said sincerely, as Lady Newfield patted her back gently. "I thank you."

"But of course." Lady Newfield reached up and pressed Julianna's cheek lightly. "Now, you must take a deep breath and step into the church, Julianna. The time to wed Lord Altringham is come."

QUITE HOW JULIANNA had made her way to the front of the church when her legs were shaking so terribly and her heart pounding in a furious manner, she could not quite say. The foreboding figure of Lord Altringham—tall, with his shoulders flat and his hands tight behind his back—awaited her arrival, but when she stood by him, he did not so much as glance at her.

Her heart twisted in her chest and she closed her eyes tightly. He did not want to marry her and she did not want to marry him. And yet, here they were and there was nothing she could do about it.

As the ceremony began, Julianna tried to recall the blessings that would soon be hers when she became Lady Altringham. Lady Newfield had told her many times that to be Lady Altringham was a blessing in itself, for she would have rank and position within society.

Julianna knew that, whilst such a thing was true in itself, it did not mean that society would show her any sort of respect or consideration. In fact, they would look at her as though she meant very little, recalling precisely what had occurred in order to force Lord Altringham's hand. Perhaps some would begin to suggest that she herself had intended such a thing from the very beginning.

You will have your own estate, she reminded herself. *You will be mistress of a very fine house. You will lack for nothing. You will not become a spinster, a governess, or a paid companion. There is no longer any shame from your father attached to you. Perhaps one day, you will bear children.*

Heat flew into her face at this thought as she glanced up at Lord Altringham. He was staring steadily forward, and she dropped her head almost at once, feeling a little afraid that he might see her watching him so. She knew nothing about Lord Altringham, she realized, save for the fact that his reputation as a rake preceded him. She had discovered as much from Lady Newfield, who knew the gentleman the moment she had laid eyes on him. Whether or not he had a cruel temper, she could not say. How relieved she was that Lady Newfield would attend with her wherever she was to go with Lord Altringham once the ceremony was over! At least she would have a little protection for a short time.

"Miss Martins?"

Her head lifted and she saw the question in the parson's eyes. Embarrassed, she dropped her head and held out her hand to her father. He took it and placed it firmly on Lord Altringham's. Julianna barely moved, feeling the coldness in Lord Altringham's hand and wondering if it reached his heart also.

Her words of promise were spoken, Lord Altringham spoke his also, and then very soon, the matter was at an end. Her veil was lifted but she did not look up into Lord

Altringham's face, certain that he would have already turned his head away. They were wed and nothing now could separate them.

The small church was entirely silent as they walked from the building. Julianna saw Lady Newfield smiling at her, clearly a sign of encouragement, but Julianna could not bring herself to smile back. Her whole body was trembling, her head bent low.

"The carriage will take you to my estate."

They were the first words Lord Altringham had ever spoken to her. Julianna looked up at him but he had turned his head away, gesturing to the carriage before her.

"Might I ask," she began, aware of just how badly her voice trembled, "whether you will attend with me?"

A harsh bark of laughter ripped from his mouth as he began to stride away. "I have no intention of going anywhere but London, *wife*," he said, the words loud and filled with anger. "Good day to you." His steps were firm and sure as he made his way toward a horse that was waiting for him, being held by a small boy. Lord Altringham threw him a coin as he looped the reins over the horse's head.

Julianna stood, frozen with shock as her new husband pulled himself up on to his horse, grasped the reins, and kicked the horse's sides. With a whinny, the horse gathered itself and broke into a gallop, dust flying up from where its hooves bit into the dirt. Julianna pressed one hand to her heart, her eyes wide with horror as she realized just what had happened. Her husband had separated himself from her almost at once, without hesitation and without even a modicum of concern for her. She was to go to his estate and remain there, until he decided, at his leisure, whether he would return.

Embarrassment and shame climbed up her spine as she dropped her head.

"Quickly now, my girl."

A firm hand caught her arm, tugging her forward gently toward Lord Altringham's carriage.

"Grandmama," Julianna whispered, feeling weak and hopeless. "He has gone back to London."

Lady Newfield's eyes flashed. "A very selfish decision indeed," she proclaimed as one of the servants opened the carriage door for her. "But nothing that can be changed now. Come now, in you go, and I shall take leave of your father for you before I join you here."

Julianna could barely breathe, her hands pressed hard against her heart as she stared, unseeingly, at the seat across from her. Lord Altringham had gone back to London rather than do his duty as he ought. He was her husband and certainly should be treating her with respect, but it seemed that he had no thoughts for anyone but himself. Relief that the church had not been particularly busy with well-wishers flung itself at her, glad that not many would see her shame. Of course, those within society would know that she had been left behind at the estate, for she highly doubted that Lord Altringham would keep such a thing to himself. No, most likely, he would laugh about it with his friends, would tell them what he had done and expect them, in return, to laugh along with him.

"Well, that is settled."

Lady Newfield climbed into the carriage with a good deal more strength than Julianna had expected, reaching up to rap on the roof. Julianna did not dare even lift her eyes to look out of the window, such was her shame, even though she knew in her heart that her father would not make any attempt to wave her off.

"It is just as well that I had my things placed with yours on the earlier carriage," Lady Newfield said briskly, sitting back and placing her hands in her lap. "Lord Altringham will not expect my company at his estate, of course, but it cannot be helped."

Julianna sniffed indelicately, her vision blurring with tears as she looked up at Lady Newfield. "He will not be present at the estate in order to complain about your company, grandmama," she said sadly. "He is, as I have told you, gone to London."

Lady Newfield shook her head, tutting for a moment. "I am sure that he will not stay away for long," she said firmly. "After all, whilst there is still some time left of the Season, he is now a married gentleman and I am sure cannot stay away from his wife for long!"

Julianna shook her head. "I have no confidence in him," she said, recalling just how sharply he had spoken to her as he had prepared to leave. "I did not even look into his face for a single moment, Grandmama, for he would not so much as look at me." Her shoulders dropped as she continued to battle tears. "I am certain that he means to have very little to do with me. Whilst he had done his duty, he will give me no time, no attention, no consideration. It is as though his life has continued on just as it has always been, whereas I shall remain in his estate without even the smallest joys at becoming his wife."

Lady Newfield said nothing for a few minutes, sitting back in her seat and searching Julianna's face. Julianna returned her gaze, her heart beating slowly and with a sense of sorrow washing over her. This was not the circumstance she had hoped to one day find herself in when she had first thought of matrimony. Rather, she had found herself hoping that the gentleman she would wed would, at the very least, care for her a little. She had never expected love, even though such a thing was the most wonderful of dreams, for Julianna had always been practical in her thoughts. And yet now to be married and to feel such pain and sadness quite broke her heart.

"Then you must write to your husband the moment we reach his estate," Lady Newfield declared. "I understand it is only a two-day drive to London from the Altringham estate, so you should have a reply from him very soon."

Spreading her hands, Julianna looked into her grandmother's face without hope. "And what am I to write?"

"Well, you must ask him just how long he intends to be in London for," Lady Newfield replied quickly, as though this was something Julianna ought to have known. Julianna dropped her head, tears touching her cheeks. "Thereafter, you will be able to determine just what you should do next."

"What I should do?" Julianna lifted her head and looked at her grandmother, a sense of foreboding filling her. "What am I to do?"

"Yes, precisely," Lady Newfield said with such a

sense of firmness that Julianna's tears began to dry on her cheeks. "You do not intend to simply do as he asked and remain at the estate, do you?"

Opening her mouth to reply that yes, this was precisely what she had intended to do, Julianna closed it again slowly and sat back a little more firmly in her chair. She narrowed her eyes and saw her grandmother smile.

Something began to warm her heart and some of the sorrow she felt so keenly began to fade away.

"What do you mean?" she asked slowly as Lady Newfield grinned broadly. "You cannot mean that I ought to return to London in order to pursue him?"

Lady Newfield's smile remained and her eyes lit up, her neatly pinned gray hair bobbing back and forward as she nodded. "That is precisely what I mean, Julianna," she said, without a note of questioning in her voice. "To remain at his estate, to do precisely as he asks without complaint, will only make both you and him quite miserable. Thus, you must do something about the situation, even though I am well aware that it is not of your making."

"No, indeed, it is not," Julianna murmured, folding her arms across her chest and allowing herself to consider all that her grandmother said. "But I do not think that searching him out in London will be a wise thing to do, Grandmama. He clearly does not want to know me, else he would have shown a little more interest in me at the first!"

Lady Newfield waved a hand as though to push aside Julianna's concerns. "It does not matter what Lord Altringham wishes, Julianna," she said firmly. "You are married now. He has a wife, you have a husband. And one way or the other, he is going to discover that you are the best thing that could ever have happened to him. I am quite certain of that."

"A note for you, my lady."

Julianna's heart quickened as she took the note from the wooden tray held out to her by the butler. It had been a fortnight since she had sent her first letter to Lord Altringham, and a fortnight of waiting for him to reply. Lady Newfield had been quite certain that a reply would come in time. Had it not been for her, Julianna was quite certain her spirits would have faded quite terribly.

"A note, you say?" Lady Newfield half rose from her chair, then sat back down again, choosing not to stand up and hurry over to her granddaughter. "Pray, what does it say, Julianna?"

Julianna glanced up at the waiting butler, quite certain she saw a glimmer of sympathy in his kind face. "I thank you. I do not require anything else for the present," she said, and he smiled, bowed, and took his leave. Julianna sat for a moment or two, looking down at the letter in her hand and feeling her whole body run wild with tension. What would it say? Would Lord Altringham be returning to his estate? Would she soon have to make preparations?

"Open it, Julianna!"

Lady Newfield's exasperated voice prompted her to

react. Quickly, she broke open Lord Altringham's wax seal, unfolding the letter quickly.

Her heart sank. This was no letter. It was merely a note. A note that one might send to another over some small matter or other.

"Julianna," Lady Newfield murmured, her eyes searching Julianna's face. "You have gone quite pale."

Taking in a deep breath and forcing herself not to cry, Julianna tried to shrug but did not manage to do anything other than lift one shoulder.

"He writes that he intends to remain in London for the foreseeable future," she said, aware of how quiet and tremulous her voice had become in only a matter of moments. "And that I should not expect his return."

For some minutes, nothing was said. Silence rose between them and Julianna felt unwilling to say anything of consequence for fear that it would only add to the distress that both she and her grandmother clearly felt.

"Well!" Lady Newfield threw herself out of her chair, beginning to stride up and down the drawing room, her skirts flying about her as she did so. "That is more than a little insulting, my dear, and I certainly do not intend to allow you to be so disrespected without taking action!"

Swallowing hard, Julianna let out a long breath. "Do you mean to return me to London, Grandmama?"

"Just as we have already spoken of, yes," Lady Newfield said decisively. "Your husband cannot simply parade around London as he has done before." She sniffed, her anger burned into every line of her face. "I have had a letter from Lady Tillsbury and she stated that it is quite ridiculous and most disconcerting to see him behave so."

Julianna blinked rapidly, her chest constricting. "She has seen Lord Altringham?"

"Indeed, she has!" Lady Newfield declared angrily. "And his behavior is *most* disgraceful. Therefore, it is to London we shall go!"

Julianna swallowed hard, her heart thumping furiously at the thought of being in Lord Altringham's presence again. What would he say when he saw her?

"I shall speak to the staff and make arrangements," Lady Newfield said before Julianna could even think to protest. "I am sure they will be quite supportive of your return to London, my dear. I have noticed that they treat you with great consideration." With a quick smile, she hurried to the door, leaving Julianna to sit in her seat alone, the note from Lord Altringham still in her lap.

The moment the door closed, Julianna leaned forward, put her head in her hands, and began to cry. It was all such a terrible mess and now it felt as though things were only going to get worse. She was living in a home she did not know, married to a gentleman she knew nothing about, and was now to return to London in what was apparently an attempt to make things better between them. Except Julianna had the sinking feeling that all it would do would be to make the situation a good deal worse.

T homas sighed contentedly and sat back in his chair, eyeing the delicious company all around him. *This* was precisely where he needed to be in order to avoid the whirling thoughts about his wife that continued to throw themselves at his mind. He did his best to forget her, of course, and that was made all the easier by the fact that he did not even know her face, but still the thoughts would linger when he did not wish them to do so.

At least here, in society, he was able to find a good many distractions from his torturous thoughts.

"Good evening, Lord Altringham!"

Thomas looked up but did not rise, recognizing Lady Steele and knowing that if he should rise, bow over her hand, and make many compliments to her, she would only take it to mean that their rather warm acquaintance of the past might be likely to continue.

He certainly did not wish it.

"Good evening, Lady Steele," he said with a small but dismissive smile, letting his gaze flit to the other side of the room as though he found someone more interesting over in that direction. "How are you this evening?"

One glance toward Lady Steele told him that his less than warm welcome had made the point he had hoped for.

"I find myself in the most excellent of company," she answered with a brittle smile. "Although, not at this very moment, unfortunately."

Thomas could not help but chuckle at her barb which, it seemed, only made Lady Steele all the more upset. She turned on her heel, her head held high and her eyes narrowed. Striding away from him, clearly affronted, Lady Steele began to speak loudly and in rather brisk tones to someone clearly more willing than he. Thomas smiled to himself, turning his head away from her and thinking to himself that he had been quite foolish to ever have pursued the lady in the first place when he knew very well that she was rather petulant.

"You have made an enemy there."

Thomas chuckled as his friend, Lord Fairfax, sat down beside him.

"You can hardly think me troubled by the loss of Lady Steele's affections and her company," he said with a shrug. "I care nothing for her, as you well know."

Lord Fairfax nodded. "I am well aware of your lack of consideration for anyone but yourself," he said, a slight note of distaste in his voice, "but I must agree with you that she is no great loss to your company. Although," he continued, before Thomas could say anything, "you should be careful of the rumors and the like she could spread about you."

Again, Thomas let out a laugh, drawing the attention of Lady Steele, who narrowed her eyes all the more.

"I think myself quite safe in that regard, Lord Fairfax, I assure you," he said with a grin. "Rumors mean nothing to me. There are always whispers surrounding me, are there not?" Shrugging, he lifted one hand in a throwaway, uncaring gesture. "It means nothing to a rake such as I."

He watched Lord Fairfax carefully as he said this, noting how his friend frowned. It was certainly an odd friendship, given that Lord Fairfax was rather upright in his behavior and would never even consider conducting himself in a manner that could be thought of as that of a rogue or a rake, whilst Thomas himself was nothing other than the latter and was, in fact, a little proud of being spoken of in such a manner.

And yet, he thought, a trifle uneasy now, he had to admit that he had lost some of his eagerness now that he had been wed. This was a matter of a little concern for him, for he had thought to come to London to continue with his life in the very same manner, only to find himself hesitating when an opportunity to steal a kiss or the like was presented to him.

"And how is your wife?"

Thomas tensed as he looked back at Lord Fairfax, taking in the man's sharp eyes and feeling himself grow uncomfortable at the question.

"I do not know," he said honestly, not wanting to pretend that he felt anything for the lady in question. "I sent her to my estate and have no intention of returning there any time soon." He shrugged. "I may remain in

London for the little Season, if not for the following year's Season also."

Lord Fairfax frowned. "You intend to stay away from your estate simply because you now have a wife?"

"Because I can manage all of my business from London and my steward does a most excellent job back at the estate," Thomas answered quickly. "I much prefer London, as you know, and I feel no desire to return home."

Again, Lord Fairfax frowned, his brows furrowing low. "And your wife?"

Thomas looked at him sharply. "What of her?"

"What are her feelings on such a decision?" he asked, leaving Thomas to frown hard at him. "She does not want you to return?"

"She has no say in the matter," Thomas replied without hesitation. "I did not want to marry her, as you well know, but had no choice but to do so."

Lord Fairfax snorted. "It was entirely your own fault," he said pointedly. "You were in your cups and kissed a lady you thought to be another. She is not the one who did anything indelicate or incorrect now, is she?" Arching one eyebrow, he glared at Thomas as though angry with him that he should feel any sort of frustration over what had happened to him. "If you had not been so foolish, you would not now find yourself in the state of matrimony that you appear to despise so greatly. Quite frankly, I believe you quite unworthy of her."

Thomas wanted to send back a harsh retort but found himself quite unable to do so. There was nothing Lord

Fairfax had said that was incorrect, and thus he had to allow the sting of what had been said to hit hard against his skin. The truth was, he *had* been far too deep in his cups, *had* been foolish in his actions, and *had* kissed a lady he had thought to be Christina—a lady of low title who had been much too free with her favors. When he had awoken in the morning, his head groggy and his throat burning with fire, he had been horrified to discover that news of his betrothal had been flying around London.

"At least you did the honorable thing and married the girl," Lord Fairfax muttered begrudgingly. "Although I do think it is very wrong of you to leave her at your estate whilst you return here."

"Come now," Thomas replied, forcing an easy smile to his face. "Surely you must know that I am not capable of doing more than one good thing at a time!" He chuckled, rising to his feet as he did so in order to remove himself from this conversation. He did not want to talk any further with Lord Fairfax for his words were becoming a little too much to bear, although Thomas was making quite certain that his friend did not know such a thing. "Do excuse me. I must go speak to Lord and Lady Forester."

He turned his back quickly on Lord Fairfax, weary of the pangs of guilt that Lord Fairfax was—either wittingly or unwittingly—forcing into his soul. He did not want to think of his wife, did not want to even recall that he *was* married. The best thing he could do was continue to enjoy all that society had to offer, without even a single consideration for her.

"Good evening, Lord Altringham!"

A broad smile settled across his face as he greeted Lady Forester, bowing first to Lord Forester and then to the lady. She was a lady always glad of his company and certainly something of a flirt, although he had never once attempted to take anything from her. A rake he was, yes, but he would not steal kisses or affections from a lady already married. Especially not when the husband was an acquaintance of Thomas'.

"And where is your dear wife?" Lady Forester asked, after some small pleasantries had been exchanged. "I was hoping very much to be introduced to her!"

A flare of irritation burned in Thomas' heart but he steeled himself with an effort, putting a smile on his face that he did not truly feel.

"Alas, she has remained at the estate," he explained, hoping that she could hear the pang of regret that he had forced into his voice. "She was quite weary and thus chose to remain for the rest of the Season."

"I am a little surprised that *you* are here, then," Lord Forester replied, not keeping his thoughts to himself in any way. "Would you not wish to be in the company of your new wife? To know her a little better rather than return to society?" He lifted one eyebrow. "Particularly after the way that you were flung together."

Thomas forced a laugh that hid his frustration. He did not want to talk of his wife. He did not want to have *others* speaking of his wife. Instead, all he wanted was merely to enjoy the evening without thought or mention of her and yet no matter where he went, he seemed dogged by her even though she was not present.

"There is plenty of time for us to know each other better, I am sure," he said with a flippant wave of his hand. "After all, marriage is not of a short duration, usually."

Lady Forester's eyes gleamed although Thomas did not know what such a thing might mean. Putting a hand on her husband's arm, she looked up at him, pulling her gaze from Thomas.

"Do not berate him just because he is not as enamored with his bride as you once were," she said, a note of teasing in her voice. "And Lord Altringham is quite right. There is a lifetime for both he and Lady Altringham to know each other better. Allow him to enjoy what is left of the Season without any such guilt being placed upon his shoulders."

Lord Forester opened his mouth to protest, only to shrug, smile at his wife, and pat her hand gently.

"Very well, I shall refrain," he said with a half-smile. "Now, I must make my excuses, Lord Altringham, for I am to take my wife to play a hand of cards."

Thomas smiled and inclined his head, turning his head in the hope that he might find *someone* within the room who would not wish to either speak of his marriage or question as to where his wife might now be. This was an evening assembly and it was meant to be nothing more than dancing, conversation, cards, and a good deal of excellent champagne—at the expense of their hosts, Lord and Lady Tillsbury—and he wanted simply to enjoy it without thought of his wife.

"Oh, do excuse me!"

He started violently, reeling back as he realized that,

in his depth of thought, he had walked directly into the path of a young lady. She had stumbled back but had, thankfully, managed to keep her feet. Her eyes caught his for just a moment, only for a quiet gasp to pull at her lips as she dropped her gaze.

"Pray, excuse me, my lady," Thomas said at once, bowing low and reaching out one hand toward her. "Might I enquire as to whether or not you are all right?" He put a warm smile on his face and looked directly into her blue eyes, using all of his charm to put her at ease. The lady blushed and looked away, her cheeks pink, and Thomas felt himself smile inwardly. There was no harm done. A little smile, some flicker of concern in his eyes, and she was already warming to him.

"I am quite well, I thank you," she said, her voice low and quiet, her eyes still darting anywhere but his face. He made to say more, only for her to tug her hand away, tendrils of fair hair bouncing around her temples as she lifted her chin. It was a little astonishing to have her react so, especially when he thought he had managed to smooth things over almost at once.

"Do excuse me."

She said nothing more but swung around on her heel and moved away from him, gliding swiftly across the floor as though some sort of ethereal spirit was within the room. Thomas frowned hard, looking after her and wondering why she did not want to linger in his company. It was very rare for a lady to remove herself from his presence in such a firm manner when they had not had too long to converse. Something like frustration bubbled up within him as he watched her walk away, his teeth gritting together hard as he fought to keep his face impassive so that no one watching him would notice his change in expression.

And yet, despite that, his hands were curling, his jaw tight. Whatever had occurred, Thomas found himself greatly irritated with the way the young lady had behaved. Yes, he had inadvertently walked into her but that was no reason to pull herself away from him as though his company were distasteful!

Shrugging, Thomas turned away and blew out a breath, trying to tell himself that he need not concern himself with such things and that he ought not to care. Setting his shoulders, he lifted his chin and made his way toward the card room, quite certain that there, at the very least, he would be able to enjoy himself without interruption.

CHAPTER THREE

"Did you see his face?"

Julianna sank down into the chair, looking at her grandmother with a heavy heart.

"I did not," Lady Newfield answered gently, leaning forward so that she might look at her granddaughter a little more carefully. "But you will recall that I was not present at the time you saw him."

Julianna did not know what to say, her stomach twisting this way and that as embarrassment seeped into her heart all over again. When Lady Tillsbury had invited both Julianna and Lady Newfield to her evening assembly—their first foray out into society since arriving in London—Julianna had already been more than a little anxious as to what would occur. She had thought she would see her husband, would greet him as warmly as she could, and explain her reappearance in London.

Instead, she had managed to be knocked back by him, given that he had accidentally walked directly into her path, and thereafter, had been both horrified and astonished to realize that he did not know who she was.

"He looked at me as though I were a complete stranger," Julianna whispered, covering her face with her hands and feeling quite wretched. "I was not known to him."

"Then the fault is his," Lady Newfield said firmly. "You have no blame in this, Julianna."

Julianna swallowed hard, only just managing to hold back her tears. She wanted to burst into floods of tears, to let her shoulders shake and her body rack with sobs, such was her shame and mortification, but with an effort, she steeled herself, took in a deep breath, and lifted her head.

"He did not even know me," she said again, as though her grandmother did not understand. "When he rested his gaze directly upon me, there was not even a flicker of recognition."

Lady Newfield let out a long, slow breath, her brow furrowed. "It is something I did not expect, I will be honest," she said. "But we must take this as best we can."

Spreading her hands, Julianna shook her head. "What is there that I can do?" she asked slowly. "Speak to Lord Altringham and inform him that the lady he walked into last evening was, in fact, his wife?" She shook her head. "I do not think I could bear the embarrassment."

"Then what else is there for us to do?" her grandmother asked gently, looking at Julianna with an open expression. "Do you wish for us to continue on as we are in the hope that one of your husband's acquaintances will inform him of the truth of your identity?"

Julianna sighed and dropped her hands, closing her eyes tightly for a moment. "I-I think we should return to the estate," she said hopelessly. "I cannot see anything else to do."

"No!" Lady Newfield's sharp response filled Julianna with surprise. Lifting her head, she was astonished to see her grandmother's face etched with anger, her brow furrowed, her cheeks coloring, and her eyes gleaming with evident fury. "No, Julianna! I will not allow you to go running back to your husband's estate in order to hide away from the difficulties that now face you. You have done enough of that already, Julianna!"

Julianna caught her breath, her eyes flaring as she looked back into her grandmother's face, seeing her in a way that she had never done before.

"I do not mean to be harsh with you, but I must tell you now, Julianna, that you must show a little more gumption."

She swallowed hard. "Gumption?" she murmured tremulously, blinking back hot tears that had sprung, unbidden, to her eyes.

"Indeed," Lady Newfield said resolutely. "Gumption. Courage. And determination and strength. Those things are what you need to find deep within yourself, my dear girl, if you are going to do what needs to be done."

Julianna let out a long breath, her shoulders lowering as she did so. Her grandmother had never spoken to her in such a way before and now to hear such fierceness from her was quite extraordinary. Indeed, she did not even know how to react.

"You have been under your father's strict rules for too long," Lady Newfield said in a much gentler tone. "You have tried your very best, I know, but your hopes have died completely, have they not?"

A single tear fell onto Julianna's cheek and she quickly brushed it away. "My father is not well-liked within society, as you well know, Grandmama," she said, her voice a little broken. "Thus, it comes as no surprise to me that my new husband wants not even to look upon me, given not only the manner of our meeting but also my father and my background."

Lady Newfield rose from her chair and walked smartly across the room toward Julianna. Reaching out, she tipped up Julianna's chin and Julianna had no other choice but to look into her grandmother's eyes, seeing the firmness in her gaze.

"I must ask you, Julianna," she began quietly. "Do your father's sins mean that you also bear the guilt and the weight of them?"

A flicker of a frown crossed her brow. "I share no guilt in my father's corrupt ways, if that is what you mean," she said, a little confused.

Lady Newfield's smile became a little sad. "Then why do you continue to behave as though you have no worth simply because of what your ridiculous and foolish father has chosen to do?"

It was a question that Julianna had never been presented with before. Her grandmother touched her cheek and then stepped away, going to ring the bell for tea. The question that her grandmother had just asked her seemed to hang about her as though a cloud of smoke surrounded her chair, holding her tightly. It was true, she realized, that she had spent her time these last few years hiding in the shadows, afraid of what her father would do next, terrified that she would sink even lower within society. She had never behaved incorrectly, had never chosen to do anything other than what society—and her father— expected. And yet, she was the one who cringed in shame, who hid in the shadows, afraid to step out into the light. Even though she knew that society did not want to look at her, did not even want to glimpse her, Julianna began to realize that it had become something of a protection for her, allowing her to hide in the way she had always done.

Of course, now she had a husband and still, she realized, she was trying to hide from everyone *including* Lord Altringham. But what else could she do? Just how much strength and courage did she have? Enough to do as Lady Newfield was pushing her to do?

"What is it that you think I should do, Grandmama?" she asked quietly as Lady Newfield dropped back into her chair, no longer appearing as angry as before. "I will try to be as courageous and as determined as you wish me to be."

Lady Newfield's smile was gentle. "It will take a great deal of strength from you, I know, but I do believe it will be for your best, my dear girl."

"I have never had anyone truly considering me in such a way before, Grandmama," Julianna answered, her eyes filling with tears—but tears of happiness rather than of sorrow. "I do want to try and improve, if you think it will help."

Lady Newfield nodded, tilting her head. "Not only for you, my dear Julianna, but also for your husband." She leaned forward in her chair, her eyes sharp. "For my intention for you is that you pull your husband toward you in a manner that will prove to him that you are of more worth than any of his other acquaintances. And for him to realize that the lady he has come to regard deeply and with perhaps even affection is, in fact, his wife."

This made Julianna frown. She could not quite understand how her husband would come to consider her in such a light when surely, she would introduce herself to him as such.

"For you are not going to be 'Lady Altringham', even though that is what you are," Lady Newfield continued, her eyes darting from one part of the room to the next, as though the plan were only just forming in her mind. "You shall be Miss Sussex."

Julianna's lips parted in surprise, a stammering sound coming from her mouth, but no full words being formed.

"And I am a friend of your parents who has begged to take you into society," Lady Newfield finished, looking quite satisfied. "Although..." Her brows furrowed and she looked back at Julianna. "Did you speak to many people last evening at the assembly? Did you inform them as to who you were?"

Such was the shock of what Lady Newfield was suggesting that it took Julianna a few seconds to react. "No. No," she said slowly, not quite certain that she liked what she was hearing. "Of course, I spoke to Lady Tillsbury but I was not introduced to anyone new and certainly none present sought out my company." It had been something of a disappointing evening, although Julianna had berated herself for believing that it might have been a little different simply because she was now Lady Altringham. And, of course, once she had seen her husband, once she had realized that he did not know who she was, she had wanted the evening to be over almost immediately.

"Then I shall have to speak to Lady Tillsbury," Lady Newfield said pensively. "But I am sure she shall be agreeable."

Julianna held her hands up. "But Grandmama," she said quickly, "you forget that I was introduced to a good few others the last time I was in society. What of them?"

Lady Newfield shrugged. "I will make certain that your appearance is so altered that they will not recognize you," she said decisively. "Now, Julianna, there is much for us to do." She eyed her keenly. "Do you have the strength and the courage to do as I have asked, believing that it will be for your best?"

It took a moment or two for Julianna to reply. Still, she was a little uncertain as to what her grandmother would ask her to do and what she fully intended, but the question still hung in the air. Did she have the courage to just trust what her grandmother had planned for her? And could she find the strength within her to step forward in the hope that her husband would know precisely who she was, in both face and character?

"Yes, Grandmama," she said, the words pulled slowly from her lips. "Yes, I believe that I do."

"Are you ready?"

Julianna let out her breath slowly as she looked at her reflection in the mirror. Her hair had been trimmed and then beautifully arranged so that a cascade of curls fell from the back of her head. Her grandmother had then insisted that she went immediately to the dressmaker to find some new gowns that were the very height of fashion, although Julianna had to admit that she was not quite certain of the color she now wore.

It was a deep, luscious blue that Lady Newfield had stated would bring out Julianna's eyes a little more, but such was the depth of color that Julianna feared it would make her rather obvious at whatever occasion they were to attend next. The long, white gloves were quite lovely, however, and of course, she would have to take her fan with her also.

"My dear!" Lady Newfield entered the dressing room with her hands clasped and her face lighting up with evident delight. "You look wonderful!"

The dressmaker stepped in behind Lady Newfield, her eyes flicking over Julianna as she cocked her head, bird-like, in order to assess her.

"I think that color does suit you very well, my lady," she said approvingly, and Lady Newfield nodded in agreement. "The color of your eyes is much more vivid, just as your companion has said."

Lady Newfield beamed. "I was quite certain that it would," she said, walking all around Julianna as though to take her in from every angle. "You will have to wear it to the ball tomorrow evening. It is quite lovely, truly." She smiled at Julianna. "*You* are quite lovely."

"I thank you," Julianna murmured, not wanting to voice her concerns now that her grandmother and the dressmaker appeared to be so contented with the gown.

"I think that will do for the present," Lady Newfield said, satisfied. "You have now three new evening gowns and two walking dresses." She smiled at the dressmaker and Julianna let out a small sigh of relief, glad that they would not insist that she try on yet another dress given that they had been doing so for some time. "Will you change?"

"Yes, of course," Julianna said gratefully. "I thank you, Grandmama."

A SHORT TIME LATER, Julianna stepped out from the dressing room and back into the main part of the shop, seeing her grandmother bending over some ribbons.

"Come and look at these," Lady Newfield said, without so much as glancing up at Julianna. "And tell me what you think."

Quickly, Julianna made her way over toward the ribbons, only for her head to come up as she heard the bell on the door chime as it opened.

Her breath caught almost at once. It was none other than Lord Altringham. Lord Altringham, who had walked into her last evening and did not recognize her. Her husband. The one gentleman she had been dreading setting eyes upon again.

Hastily, Julianna dropped her eyes back to the ribbons, but it appeared she was much too late.

"Good afternoon!" Lord Altringham boomed, his voice filling the shop, and he strode across the floor toward her. "My lady." He bowed low, sweeping forward and making a most elaborate show. "You disappeared last evening without permitting me to know your name, my lady, and I simply cannot allow such a situation to continue, not when I made such a fool of myself."

Julianna darted a glance toward her grandmother, who straightened, turned, and looked Lord Altringham full in the face. There was something of a risk in it, for Lord Altringham, whilst having never been formally introduced to Lady Newfield given his desire to stay far from Julianna herself, had been told of her connection to the family by Julianna's father.

"Lord Altringham," he said, bowing again to Lady Newfield. "I must beg your pardon for my lack of consideration and less than appropriate introduction, but the circumstances in which we met," he sent a quick glance toward Julianna, "were less than agreeable."

Lady Newfield smiled but Julianna noticed that it did not reach her eyes.

"Indeed," she said, bobbing a quick curtsy. "Might I then introduce myself as Lady Newfield?" Lifting her chin, she looked into his face and Julianna's hands tightened as she held them in front of her, her fingers laced together. She wanted to see if there was any flicker of recognition in Lord Altringham's face, but as she watched his hazel eyes take in Lady Newfield, she saw nothing of the sort.

"My lady," Lord Altringham murmured, bowing. "And might you be so good as to introduce this young lady to me?" His eyes turned back to Julianna, lingering on her for a greater length of time than ever before. He was smiling at her too, something she had never seen on his face when he had been in her company before.

"But of course," Lady Newfield said quickly. "Might I present Miss Sussex? I am a friend of the family and begged to take her to London for the Season this year."

Julianna noticed that her grandmother made no mention of any particular father or mother in her introduction but quickly sank into a curtsy, keeping her eyes low as she rose. There was a bit of heat in her cheeks now and she did not want Lord Altringham to think that she was reacting to his charms.

"Miss Sussex," Lord Altringham said with such a warmth to his voice that Julianna could not help but look up at him, her surprise perhaps evident on her face, for his smile broadened as she watched him. "I am very glad to make your acquaintance. I am also very sorry for walking into you last evening. It was entirely my fault and I can only beg your forgiveness."

She gave him a small smile but did not keep her gaze on his face, finding his presence to be quite overwhelming. He was so very different from how he had been on their wedding day and she found the change to be quite astonishing. There was no hardness in his face now, no burning anger in his voice. No sneer touched the corner of his mouth, no furious fire alight in his eyes. Instead, he was all smiles and delight, trying to make her warm to him, to make her glad to be in his presence.

"You do not forgive me?"

Her face burned and she darted her eyes to his, her smile a trifle disingenuous. "But of course," she said, her voice low and quiet. "It was an accident, nothing more."

"You are most kind." Lord Altringham bowed low but Julianna did not curtsy. She felt overcome in his presence, finding him to be a very strong character that threatened to overwhelm her should she allow it. There was a moment of silence, silence that Julianna felt to be rather awkward, with Lord Altringham now clearing his throat.

"Might I ask if you are attending Lord Irvingshire's ball tomorrow evening?"

Julianna glanced toward her grandmother, seeing the tiny nod and trying to put a smile back on her face.

"We are, yes," she said, and Lord Altringham beamed at her, evidently filled with delight that this was to occur. "And you?"

"Yes, yes, of course," he said, waving a hand as though she ought to expect that his attendance was a given. "Then I must hope, Miss Sussex, that we will be able to dance together at the ball. I shall, with your permission, seek you out tomorrow evening so I can write my name on your dance card."

Her throat constricted, her heart hammering at the thought of being in her husband's arms without his awareness of her true identity. Knowing she could not speak to confirm such a thing, she merely forced a smile and curtsied, hoping that this would be enough to satisfy him for his answer.

Evidently, it was.

"Capital!" Lord Altringham boomed, bowing low. "I

shall let you return to your ribbons now, of course. Thank you for the introductions, Lady Newfield, and Miss Sussex..." He smiled at her, his eyes fixed to hers, and Julianna again felt her heart thump furiously. "I look forward to tomorrow evening when we are to meet again."

CHAPTER FOUR

"You are in good spirits this evening, Lord Altringham."

Thomas grinned as he bowed to Lord Fairfax. "You did not expect me to be in such a good state?" he asked, lifting one eyebrow. "Or is it that you did not think I would be in a happy mood since my dear wife is not present?"

Lord Fairfax rolled his eyes, his smile tilting to one side. "Very well, I shall not suggest such a thing or even speak of your wife again, if that is what you wish."

"I *do* wish it," Thomas said firmly, not holding back from his friend. "I am determined to enjoy the rest of the Season even without her company." He saw his friend sigh but nod, allowing a sense of relief to wash over him as he did so. There was nothing he wanted to think about in terms of his wife for fear that it would take away from the enjoyment of this evening. Already, he had seen and spoken to a number of acquaintances, as well as one or two young ladies who had passed him some very warm glances indeed.

He chuckled to himself, shaking his head as he did so. They were all very eager for his company and it made his delight at being back in society grow all the more. The way the ladies looked at him, the knowledge that so many would simply melt into his arms if he danced with them, and the awareness that there was much willingness on the part of the ladies simply added to his arrogance and pride, puffing out his chest a little more with every smile he saw.

"You are, no doubt, going to make the best of the gardens this evening," Lord Fairfax said with a wry smile. "The only question is which of the ladies present this evening will be the first to garner your attentions?"

Thomas chuckled, glad that his friend had decided to stop asking about Lady Altringham and instead converse as they usually did. "I cannot imagine what you mean," he said, feigning injury. "If I am to walk in the gardens, it will simply be because of the need for fresh air in what is bound to be a very warm evening indeed." With a sly glance, he chuckled loudly. "Besides which, I intend to go and see Lady Guthrie tomorrow afternoon."

Lord Fairfax laughed harshly, a slightly angry tone to his laugh. "You are always able to have whatever you wish, are you not, Lord Altringham?" he said with a shake of his head. "I should feel sorry for the young ladies that you set your eyes on, but I cannot for I know that they go with you willingly."

Thomas put one hand on his heart and tried to look shocked. "I should never take a lady out for a short stroll in the gardens if she was not willing," he said, although the truth, he knew, was that he was well able to encourage a lady who might be a little reluctant to do so. "And besides which, is it not expected that I behave in such a way?" He grinned as he let his gaze trail across the room. "In fact, I am sure that if I did *not* do such a thing as you have suggested, then there would be shock and disappointment within the *ton*."

Lord Fairfax shook his head. "I must pray that you find a lady unwilling to bend to your flattery and your charms," he said, rather grumpily. "Perhaps that will make your arrogance begin to die away somewhat."

Thomas merely laughed, only for his eyes to fix upon a young lady in a blue gown which shimmered slightly as she moved. Her face was rather anxious, her eyes wide as she looked out across the ballroom, her gloved hands held tightly in front of her.

Thomas let a small smile tug across his lips as he watched her. She was not beautiful by any means, certainly not a diamond of the first water, but this was now the third time he had seen her and there was something about her that seemed to draw him toward her. She was elegant and graceful, which he certainly appreciated, but perhaps it was that reluctance in her manner, the hesitation that had her looking to Lady Newfield in almost every moment that passed, but for whatever reason, he could not help but want to go to her almost at once.

He did not, however. To rush toward her with long strides, to make himself so obvious and persistent, was not a wise idea. He had to take his time, to make sure that his meeting her was done carefully and with great precision, so that the *ton* would not notice any sort of interest on his part.

"Might I enquire as to which young lady has captured your attentions?"

Thomas turned his head back to Lord Fairfax, noting the flicker of interest in his friend's eyes and finding himself more than a little reluctant to say anything at all.

"You are quite mistaken," he said with a chuckle. "There is no one in particular. There are plenty of young ladies here this evening. I was merely assessing which ones might be worth my time."

Thankfully, he was spared any more questions by the arrival of the widowed but lovely Lady Darlington, who came to stand directly in his path, curtsying beautifully but keeping her head up and her eyes looking into his without hesitation or demureness.

"Good evening, Lord Altringham," she purred, not even glancing toward Lord Fairfax. "How very glad I am to see you this evening."

"Lady Darlington," he replied, bowing warmly. "I do hope you are dancing this evening? I should very much like to steal the waltz from you."

She laughed and held out her ribboned dance card to him, her eyes glowing with evident delight as she watched him peruse the dances. He quickly wrote his name down for the country dance and the waltz.

"Wonderful," she murmured as he handed it back to her with a warm smile, knowing that the waltz might lead to something a little more. "I do hope that you will not sign up your name to the quadrille, Lord Altringham, for it comes directly after the waltz and I should like to keep you in my company for a short time thereafter."

He grinned at her, knowing precisely what she meant. "I would be glad to keep that particular dance free, my lady. I look forward to your company later this evening."

As she walked away, Thomas heard Lord Fairfax sigh heavily, evidencing his displeasure at Thomas' plans.

"You must excuse me," Thomas said quickly, feeling himself growing a little weary of Lord Fairfax's censure, whether spoken or unspoken. If Lord Fairfax did not want to enjoy the warm company of a lady, then that was entirely his choice. Whereas he, himself, wanted to do precisely that and was well able to do so.

"Going to find more young ladies to *dance* with, no doubt."

"Indeed," Thomas said without hesitation. "Do enjoy your evening, Lord Fairfax."

"I am sure I shall," came Lord Fairfax's voice as Thomas turned away and began to walk away, leaving Lord Fairfax far behind. He smiled and inclined his head to many ladies as he walked, as well as to some gentlemen, of course, but there were a few that he made quite certain to ignore. The ladies he did not greet were those who were with their husbands, or who were clutching the arm of the gentleman they walked alongside with. He would not intrude on a marriage or even a courtship, even if he was given the option to do so. Yes, he was a rake, but he had some principles—and principles he prided himself on.

"Good evening, Lord Altringham."

Within a few minutes of greeting Lady Smythe, Thomas found himself practically surrounded by ladies of the *beau monde*. When he requested the dance card from one, he was presented with not only the one he had asked for, but also many others from those who stood near to him. They did not wait for him to enquire as to whether or not they had a dance free that he might occupy but rather held out their cards with the expectation that he would want to dance with them. Thomas felt his chest puff out a little with pride as he took one card after the other, knowing in his mind which ladies he might steal out to the gardens with for a short time and which ones he ought to make certain to return to their companions or mothers.

And then, he recalled Miss Sussex.

His heart sank as he realized that he had written his name down for almost every dance. Pulling out his own dance card—to remind him who he was to dance with next as well as to advise him which ones were still remaining—he realized that he had only one dance left.

The quadrille. The quadrille he had promised to keep free so that Lady Darlington and he could share a little more time together thereafter. Was he willing to give that up so that he might take Miss Sussex onto the dance floor?

Thomas sighed and shook his head. No. He did not feel the urge to know Miss Sussex better to the point that he would give up a few warm moments with Lady Darlington. To even consider such a thing was quite ridiculous.

"Good evening, Lord Altringham."

He looked up from his card to see none other than the lady of his thoughts now standing in front of him. He was rather surprised that Miss Sussex had come to greet him of her own accord, given just how demure and quiet she had appeared during his two other conversations with her, but perhaps the music of the ball and the liveliness of the dancers had emboldened her somewhat.

"Good evening, Miss Sussex," he said, noting Lady Newfield standing only a foot or so away. He nodded to her, seeing the tiny smile touch the corner of her mouth as she nodded back. Clearly, Lady Newfield knew of his reputation and was being very careful in watching her charge and whom she engaged with.

Miss Sussex's cheeks were infused with color, although whether or not that came from his company or merely being at the ball itself, Thomas did not know.

"You wished to dance with me this evening, I believe," Miss Sussex said, her blue eyes a little unsteady as she tried to look at him. They held his gaze for a moment, then dropped to his shoulder. "I thought to come and seek you out before my card is filled completely."

"I see." Thomas cleared his throat and took her card from her, still a little taken aback by her boldness. "That is quite correct, Miss Sussex, of course. I did ask to dance with you this evening." Looking down her card, he was all the more astonished to discover that her dance card was rather full. Miss Sussex was not, as far as he knew, anyone of particular merit, although clearly with being in the charge of Lady Newfield, she was of the same social standing as the lady. He, being an earl, ought really to be seeking out daughters of earls or marquesses, but there was clearly something about Miss Sussex that others recognized given that they were so eager to fill up her dance card. The ball had only been in full swing for an hour or so and he had not expected her to have so many dances taken already. The first two had already been danced and the third would begin in a few minutes. He did not have a lot of time.

"Do you see none that you like?" she asked, a small note of teasing in her voice. "Or is it that you do not wish to dance with me any longer?"

Darting his gaze up toward her, Thomas found himself smiling back at her, wondering why he found her so interesting when she was not a particular beauty. "I am sure I can find one dance to suit us both," he said, feeling himself pushing back against this strange interest in her. "After all, Miss Sussex, I fear that I am also very much engaged this evening."

Her face fell, the smile sliding from her face. "Oh, of course."

"I do still have the quadrille," he said slowly, feeling himself pulled in one direction and then the next. On one hand, he had the joy and the pleasure of Lady Darlington's company, but on the other, the dance he had promised to Miss Sussex.

"And yet you seem less than eager to take it," she said, her tone now a little unfriendly. "You have someone else in mind for that, perhaps?"

His brows rose as he looked at her, seeing the flash of anger in her eyes. Before he could tell her otherwise, before he could do anything more, Miss Sussex, it seemed, made a quick decision. To his astonishment, she pulled the card from his fingers and gave him a quick bob of a curtsy. "Then you must excuse me, Lord Altringham. I would not have you pulled from any of your other partners, given that they are all of greater importance." She turned on her heel and left his side almost immediately, with Lady Newfield's eyebrows lifting high as she watched her charge walk away. Thomas frowned hard, watching her leave and questioning why he felt no sense of relief in what she had done. It now meant that he could spend the time of the quadrille dance with Lady Darlington, which was, he told himself, precisely what he had wished for.

～

"THAT WAS AN *EXCELLENT* DANCE, LADY DARLINGTON."

She simpered up at him, her eyes bright and a small, knowing smile tugging at the corner of her mouth. "Indeed," she purred, her hand tight on his arm. "I enjoyed it very much."

Thomas kept the frown from his face with an effort. He had never once felt such a guilt over turning a lady away before, and yet now, even though he was with Lady Darlington, the only person occupying his thoughts was Miss Sussex.

"You do not look pleased, Lord Altringham," Lady Darlington cooed, looking up at him with bright eyes. "Is there something about my company that displeases you?"

Clearing his throat, he smiled at her and tried to

laugh. "Indeed not, Lady Darlington," he said, leaning down toward her meaningfully. "I am very glad indeed to be in your company."

"You are not considering Lady Guthrie at this moment, I hope?" Lady Darlington's voice had become a little cooler now, her eyes narrowed. "I know that she, too, is a favorite of yours."

Thomas lifted her hand and pressed his lips to it. "I think only of you, Lady Darlington," he said, not wanting the lady to pull away from him now. "Truly, there is no other lovelier than you."

"Good," Lady Darlington murmured, leading him toward the open door that led to the gardens—the dark, secretive gardens where many a kiss could be stolen by a gentleman who dared to try it. "Perhaps you will bring me a gift next time we meet."

A little surprised, Thomas glanced at her. "A gift?"

"Indeed," Lady Darlington laughed, although there was still a seriousness in her eyes that did not fade. "I am sure you purchase gifts for others but I, as yet, have been given nothing from you." She sighed heavily, one hand against her heart as though his lack of attention pained her. "Indeed, it has been much too long since we have been together, Lord Altringham. I am sure I have been pining for you!"

A small, lackluster smile crossed his lips, no spark of excitement flooding him despite his best efforts. Her changeability was becoming a little boring. "I see," he said, making Lady Darlington frown as she looked up at him.

"You have not pined for me, I presume," she said a

little tartly as she narrowed her eyes and looked up at him. "Is that what you are trying to say by such a remark, Lord Altringham?"

Thomas tried to collect himself, tried to smile and find his usual charms so as to set her back into a warm and contented state. "No indeed, Lady Darlington," he said, patting her hand and giving her what he hoped was a knowing look. "I have not pined for you. I have *ached* for you." Their steps became a little slower as they drew near to the doors, with Lady Darlington guiding them into the shadows by the door rather than stepping outside. "I have *yearned* for you. And now to be in your company again, it is the fulfillment of every desire I have held within me for so long."

This, thankfully, seemed to content Lady Darlington for she let out a soft laugh and pressed her hands flat against his chest, looking up at him with dark eyes. Thomas pressed all thoughts of Miss Sussex away from him, lapping up Lady Darlington's presence and feeling his heart begin to beat a little quicker with the promise in her eyes.

"Can you only linger until the end of the quadrille?" she murmured, reaching up to run her fingers lightly down his cheek. "Or might you wish to join me later this evening?"

He pressed his hand over hers, trapping it against his cheek. "I should very much like to—"

Someone caught his attention. Out of the corner of his eye, he saw none other than Miss Sussex standing, stock-still, staring at him with a horrified expression on her face. He had thought himself well hidden in shadow, but evidently, it had not been dark enough to conceal him completely. Lady Darlington did not notice Miss Sussex or Lady Newfield, who had come to stand beside her, given that her back was to them, but Thomas felt the full force of their stares.

"Lord Altringham?"

It was as though he were fixed to the spot. Staring at Miss Sussex, unable to drag his eyes away, he felt his heart pound furiously and his mouth go dry. He could not speak. He could not move. All he could do was stare back at Miss Sussex, knowing now that she saw the full reason for his reluctance to dance with her in the quadrille. In his foolishness, he had not thought that she, too, would be without a partner in the quadrille and had presumed she would be dancing, but it seemed he was quite incorrect in that matter.

Lady Newfield said something to Miss Sussex, her hand tight on her arm, and slowly, Miss Sussex turned away. Lady Newfield linked her arm though that of her charge and together, they walked away from Thomas and Lady Darlington.

"I do not know what is the matter with you this evening!" Lady Darlington huffed, pulling back from him, her hands now planted on her hips, her eyes narrowed. "You are behaving in a most ridiculous and uncertain manner and I simply cannot understand what is going on."

Thomas tried to protest, tried to explain, but it was clearly much too late. Lady Darlington threw her hands up in frustration and stepped away from him, leaving Thomas to stand alone in the shadows.

He waited there alone, expecting to feel irritation at Lady Darlington's departure and anger toward Miss Sussex for her interruption of what had been a most enjoyable moment, but instead, all he felt was a slow, burning sense of shame.

Thomas did not like it. It was not a sensation he was used to and certainly not one he liked. There was no reason for such a feeling, he told himself. He did not owe Miss Sussex anything and she herself meant nothing to him! Why now should he feel such a strange sense of guilt?

His lip curling, Thomas turned and strode through the ballroom, his face black with anger. Anger at how he felt, anger at this unwanted and unmerited sense of shame. Anger that a lady who was neither beautiful nor engaging had caught him in such a strange fashion. And anger, most of all, at his own foolish behavior in throwing aside the delectable Lady Darlington.

It was all most frustrating.

CHAPTER FIVE

Julianna tried her best to keep her spirits up, to find her courage and her strength as her grandmother had encouraged her to do, but the difficulty of seeing her husband entangled with another lady was rather hard to bear.

"You are doing very well, Julianna," her grandmother murmured as they walked through Hyde Park, greeting various ladies and gentlemen whom her grandmother appeared to know. Julianna did not know very many of them at all, or if she did recall their faces, she did not remember their names. Her mind was much too caught up with what she had seen last evening, her heart sinking into her toes as she thought of it again.

To see a lady draped against Lord Altringham had been a sword to her heart. She had been foolish enough to forget that her husband was nothing more than a rake, reminding herself, as her grandmother led her away, that this was entirely to be expected, and yet it had injured her more than she wanted to admit. The courage it had taken to go up to Lord Altringham in the first place had been difficult enough, but to first of all find herself snubbed in place of someone unknown—for Lord Altringham's disinclination to give her the quadrille had been apparent—and then see him with yet another young lady only drove the pain into her heart all the harder.

"Good afternoon, Lady Newfield."

Julianna looked up to see Lady Tillsbury and her daughter, a lady she had been introduced to once before, approaching them. Lady Tillsbury had a warm smile on her face and the young lady was watching Julianna with interest.

Julianna flushed at the scrutiny. No doubt the lady knew full well of what Julianna was doing, given that her mother had needed to be informed by Lady Newfield of Julianna's new identity.

"Good afternoon, Miss Sussex."

"Miss *Sussex*," the young lady repeated, giving Julianna a warm smile. "You see, Miss Sussex, I have not forgotten."

Julianna smiled back, albeit rather tentatively, trying to recall the lady's name. "You are very kind."

"Indeed you are, Miss Glover," Lady Newfield said, throwing Julianna a quick glance as though she knew that she had struggled to recall the lady's name. "You and your mother are the only two in all of London who know of Julianna's true identity."

Julianna's gut twisted. "It appears I am quite forget-table," she said, a little regretfully. "No one else in all of London seems to recall my true name."

"And not even your husband!" Miss Glover

exclaimed, one hand at her heart. "That is most unfortunate and certainly quite ridiculous, Miss Sussex. I am sure that must be very trying for you."

Trying to keep her composure, Julianna inclined her head but dropped her gaze to the ground. Because of this, she did not see the sharp look that Lady Tillsbury sent toward her daughter, or the way that Miss Glover dropped her head.

"Pray, Miss Sussex, will you not walk with me for a time?" Miss Glover asked suddenly, as Julianna lifted her gaze back to the lady. "I am sure my mother and your grandmother would like to converse for a time and I should very much like to acquaint myself with you a little better."

Such was the sweetness of her request and the genuine look in her eyes that Julianna found herself unable to refuse. Nodding but not saying a word given that she did not trust her voice, Julianna walked toward the girl, who turned about and began to walk alongside her, so that Lady Newfield and Lady Tillsbury might walk behind.

"I am sorry if I upset you just now," Miss Glover said at once, looking keenly at Julianna, who was a little surprised at how bold the lady was with her apology. "It was rather carelessly spoken and I do apologize."

Blinking in surprise, Julianna felt a smile playing about her mouth, finding herself rather enamored by this young lady. "You are very kind to say so, Miss Glover," she said quietly. "I am grateful for your consideration."

"I should *very* much like to be your friend," Miss

Glover continued, in as open a manner as before. "You are quite mysterious, if I might be permitted to say so!"

A little surprised at this, Julianna laughed and Miss Glover smiled. "I do not feel mysterious at all."

"Oh, but you are," Miss Glover said firmly as they moved a good deal more quickly along the path than Lady Newfield and Lady Tillsbury. "I find myself quite honored to meet you and to know of your circumstances —although they must be dreadfully difficult, of course."

Julianna found herself liking Miss Glover immensely. She had only been introduced to her at the evening assembly some days ago and had not had much of an opportunity to talk, but now that she was doing so, she found the lady to be warm and friendly, albeit with a rather blunt manner of speaking. Julianna did not think she had met anyone like her—aside from Lady Newfield, of course.

"I do hope that Lord Altringham returns to you with shame and disgrace once he realizes who you are," Miss Glover continued, linking arms with Julianna without so much as asking her if she wished to walk arm in arm. "I think you are incredibly brave, Miss Sussex, to do what you are doing at present," she finished with a shake of her head. "I should like to help in whatever way I can."

"That is very kind of you," Julianna said, rather over-whelmed and humbled by the lady's wish. "I do not know what to say, truth be told, for I am not even certain what it is I am to do next!"

Miss Glover laughed, pressing Julianna's arm. "Then that is precisely what I shall do first in order to help you," she declared. "What is it that—oh!"

Being dragged to a sudden stop, Julianna looked all about her to see what it was that her new friend was now gaping at, only to see, much to her shock, that the very gentleman in question was just now alighting from a carriage a little away from them. In the instant she saw him, her whole body reacted in a most uncomfortable fashion. Her legs became weak, her shoulders slumped, and her stomach began to churn. Turning her face away in an attempt to hide her face from him, she saw Miss Glover looking at her with interest.

"You are afraid of him?" she queried, but Julianna shook her head.

"Not afraid, no," she answered slowly. "I think, instead, I am a little afraid of my own reaction to him." Shrugging, she tried to explain herself. "I have no courage. I have no determination or any great strength of character. Instead, I am fearful and uncertain. I have spent a lifetime being filled with such feelings and to try and change them now has been rather difficult indeed. And then, when I do try to show some strength of will, I find that even with such confidence, my husband still will not think well of me." Some hot tears filled her eyes but Julianna blinked them away quickly. "It is foolish to think that just because I might have a little confidence, he would then seek me out or put me before his own wishes and attentions. Instead, I was swiftly reminded that he is nothing more than a rake and has no desire to change such behavior."

Miss Glover frowned, watching the way that Lord Altringham made his way toward another gentleman and two ladies who were standing together. "He is very arrogant, Miss Sussex, I will say that." She shot Julianna a sidelong glance. "I do hope that does not injure you."

Julianna laughed, her tears gone. "No, indeed not," she answered honestly. "Not when I am aware it is the truth. I..." Her mouth suddenly went dry as she stared out at Lord Altringham, noting how someone was moving toward his carriage, looking directly at him but seemingly not inclined to hurry quickly toward him.

"What is it?" Miss Glover asked as Julianna's grandmother and Lady Tillsbury joined them. "Is something wrong?"

"I am not certain," Julianna murmured quietly. "I-I can see a figure approaching Lord Altringham but in a very slow manner. It is as if he does not want to be seen. He... good gracious!"

Miss Glover had seen it also. "He has stopped his approach and climbed into Lord Altringham's carriage!" she exclaimed, sounding rather horrified. "That is quite improper. We must go to it at once." Making to stride forward, she was quickly restrained by the warning hand of her mother.

"Wait a moment, Henrietta," Lady Tillsbury said quickly. "The gentleman might very well *know* Lord Altringham and has climbed in to await a meeting with him or some such thing."

Julianna bit her lip, entirely uncertain as to what ought to be done. There was, of course, every possibility that what Lady Tillsbury had suggested was the truth of the matter, but by the way she had seen the man lurking near the carriage and climbing in with such a surreptitious manner, she feared it was not so.

"What do you think, Julianna?"

Turning her head, Julianna saw her grandmother looking at her carefully, a small gleam in her eye. It was clear that she wanted to know the truth of what Julianna thought and was encouraging her to speak openly.

"I-I think," Julianna said, a little embarrassed to see everyone's eye on her, "that there is something untoward about this situation." She swallowed hard, trying to set aside all of her feelings as to what had happened before as regarded Lord Altringham and seeking to bolster the little courage she had. "I-I think I should like to speak to Lord Altringham to ensure that he knows what has happened and that he is fully aware of it."

Lady Newfield nodded in agreement. "A good suggestion," she said resolutely. "Well, then, Julianna, might I suggest you do as you have said? We shall remain here and watch the carriage with a firm eye."

Julianna swallowed hard, opening her mouth to protest and to state that she did not want to go to speak to Lord Altringham alone, only to see the sharp look in her grandmother's eye. There was to be no excuse now. Whether she wished to go alone or not, Julianna knew that her grandmother wanted her to do precisely as she had suggested without hesitation.

"We will be able to see you from here, so it will be all quite proper," Lady Newfield finished as Lady Tillsbury frowned hard, her eyes fixed on Lord Altringham's carriage. "Do hurry, Julianna, before it is too late!"

Julianna nodded, took in a deep breath, and forced herself to take a single step forward. Her heart was in her throat as she walked slowly toward Lord Altringham, aware that he might not only reject the opportunity to speak to her but might, in fact, simply ignore her presence entirely. After the way he had looked back at her last evening after she had stared at him as he had been in Lady Darlington's company, Julianna was not at all sure what to expect.

The moment she drew near to Lord Altringham, Julianna felt as though she had made a dreadful mistake. He was now standing between the two ladies and one had her arm linked with his, with her other hand pressed to his arm as though she could not even stand without his strength to aid her. She hesitated, coming to a slow stop a few steps away from them, not quite certain what she ought to do next. Ought she just to approach him directly? She was not sure she had the confidence for that but neither did she want to turn around and look toward Lady Newfield for assistance. Most likely, her grandmother would merely chivvy her forward with a wave of her hand.

"Miss Sussex?"

Lifting her head, she saw one of the ladies greeting her, although she did not remove herself from Lord Altringham's company.

"Good afternoon, Miss Salisbury," Julianna answered, relieved that, for once, she had remembered the name of the lady speaking to her. "I do beg your pardon for intruding in your conversation but—"

"That is quite all right," Miss Salisbury interrupted, waving a hand. "You *do* know everyone here, do you not? No?" She looked a little surprised, then laughed. "Then permit me to make the introductions."

There was no time for such things, Julianna thought, but could not find the courage to interrupt the lady in order to speak directly to Lord Altringham. Thus, she was forced, in her own weakness, to wait until Miss Salisbury had made all the introductions before she was able to say what she had intended.

"Lord Altringham," she said, a little breathlessly, such was her nerves. "I-I must ask you if you will give me a moment of your time."

Lord Altringham, who had thus far said very little save for a murmured, "Good afternoon", looked at her askance.

"It is about something of a grave matter," she continued quickly, "else I would not be so rude as to pull you away from your companions without explanation."

After a moment or two, Lord Altringham cleared his throat, nodded, and then came toward her, whilst Miss Salisbury and the others looked on with interest. Julianna fell into step with him at once, although he walked a little too quickly for her. Her mouth was dry, her brow furrowed as she tried to find the words to explain what she feared, but the only thing that came to mind was an image of the lady and Lord Altringham as they had been last evening.

Realizing with a start that they had drawn very close to the carriage, Julianna reacted swiftly, putting one hand on Lord Altringham's arm and pulling him back before she could even think of what else she ought to do.

Lord Altringham looked down at her with surprise.

"Forgive me," she mumbled, pulling her hand away at once as though she had been burned. "I mean to—"

"I had no intention of pulling you into the carriage, if that is what you feared," he said a little dryly, his eyes searching her face. "In fact, I will confess that I am surprised you are even here conversing with me after last evening's fiasco."

Choosing to ignore this, Julianna took in a deep breath and tried to speak calmly. "There is someone in your carriage, Lord Altringham." With a great effort, she looked up into his face and held his gaze. She saw his expression change at once, his brows furrowing and the sardonic smile that had graced his lips only moments before now beginning to fade. She forced herself to continue. "Were you expecting someone?"

"What do you mean that someone has climbed into my carriage?" Lord Altringham said, frowning hard. "What can you mean by such a remark?"

Pressing her lips together for a moment, Julianna tried to explain without making herself sound too ridiculous. "I have been out walking with a... a friend," she said, gesturing to where Miss Glover and the other two ladies were now waiting. "As we walked, we saw someone climb into your carriage in a most surreptitious manner. Your driver did not even take notice!"

He held her gaze, his brows low and his hazel eyes fixed to hers. She felt as though he were looking into her very soul, as though he were searching all through her to see if she was telling the truth.

"I am not expecting anyone, no," he said, his brows lifting for a moment as a new lightness filled his face. "Although, it was mayhap a lady who did so?" Something in his eyes sparkled but Julianna found no mirth in his remark. Rather, for the very first time, she felt something akin to anger.

"I am *certain* it was a gentleman," she said with a good deal more firmness to her voice than she had first intended. "As much as you might not wish it to be so, Lord Altringham, I am quite certain that it was a gentleman who entered your carriage." She lifted one eyebrow and looked at him directly. "You do not have anything in the carriage that would be worth stealing, I hope?"

Lord Altringham's countenance changed at once. With a gasp, he bustled past her and hurried toward the carriage, his face taut and eyes wide with horror. Julianna could only watch as he threw open the door, the driver uncertain as to whether or not he ought to be preparing to leave. Glancing at her grandmother, Julianna beckoned her toward her and, with relief, saw that all three ladies were coming to her at once. Their steps were hurried, their eyes wide, and Julianna could see the look of shock on her grandmother's face. Evidently, Lady Newfield had not thought the threat to be real.

"Whatever is it?" her grandmother cried, her hands tight on Julianna's arm. "Is there some real danger?"

Julianna nodded, her throat constricting. "I do not know what it can be but Lord Altringham disappeared without barely a moment's notice after I asked if there was something within the carriage that might be worth stealing."

She was about to say more but was cut off by a shout of dismay coming from the carriage, with Lord Altringham appearing only a moment later.

"It is gone," he gasped, his hat no longer upon his head but held tightly in his hand as he waved his arms about. "I cannot quite believe it. It is gone." His face was red, his eyes looking all over Hyde Park as though he might find the perpetrator. Julianna knew it was quite impossible, for the fashionable hour was now close at hand and the park was already filling with members of the *beau monde*.

"What is gone, Lord Altringham?" Lady Tillsbury asked, taking a small step forward whilst Miss Glover exchanged an astonished glance with Julianna. "Has something been taken from you?"

Lord Altringham ran one hand through his brown hair, making his appearance a little less distinguished than before. Julianna had never seen him in such a state as he was at present, for he had always been composed, even when he had been furious with anger. His square jaw was tight, his reddened cheeks now turning scarlet as his eyes narrowed, darting still from place to place. With his hair askew and his hands flapping wildly as he muttered under his breath, he appeared almost mad with ire.

"What has been taken, Lord Altringham?" Lady Tillsbury asked again, frowning hard. "You appear quite distressed, truly."

Lord Altringham stopped short, turning to face Lady Tillsbury as though he had only just seen her.

"Yes, yes indeed," he murmured, the color beginning to drain from his face. "Yes, something has been taken. Something of great value."

Julianna found herself stepping closer, without

having intended to do so. "What was it?" she asked, finding her curiosity piqued. What could it be that had Lord Altringham so distressed? She had never seen him in such a state and to have him as such now was both intriguing and a little troubling.

However, it seemed Lord Altringham was not inclined to tell them what had been taken. He did not immediately answer and when he did, it was with a lowering of his head and a shying away of his gaze.

"It was an expensive gift," he muttered, not looking at them. "A gift that I was to give to someone on my return from Hyde Park."

Julianna saw the way that Miss Glover narrowed her eyes, just as a spot of color came into each cheek. Lady Tillsbury tutted loudly and looked at Lady Newfield with an arched brow, which Julianna took to mean that they were all aware of what this description meant, whilst she certainly did not.

"Then you must ask yourself who knew of such a *gift*," Lady Tillsbury said quickly, turning around to return to her daughter. "Come, Henrietta. It is time for us to take our leave of Lord Altringham."

Blinking in surprise, Julianna turned her head to see her own grandmother beckoning her also. Throwing a quick glance back at Lord Altringham, she was surprised to see a look of desperation on his face, as though he were afraid to be left alone with this puzzle.

Lady Newfield put a gentle hand on Julianna's arm. "We must depart also, Lord Altringham. I do apologize." Her smile was tight and did not reach her eyes. "I do hope you can solve the mystery of whoever has stolen your gift from you. Good afternoon."

Julianna did not have any opportunity to say anything more to Lord Altringham, surprised at herself when she realized there was a desire within her to do precisely that. The look they held was broken by Lady Newfield tugging Julianna quickly away, forcing her to turn around and leave Lord Altringham standing alone.

"What was it that he spoke of, Grandmama?" she asked, her breath coming quickly as she hurried along beside her grandmother. "I do not understand. Why is there so much distaste apparent on all of your faces?"

Lady Newfield stopped suddenly, looking up into Julianna's face with what appeared to be a look of deep sadness. "I do not want to tell you, Julianna, for fear that it will injure you."

Julianna steeled herself, lifting her chin as she tightened her hands into fists. "I am prepared, Grandmama."

Sighing, Lady Newfield reached out and pressed her shoulder. "Most gentlemen, when they go to visit their mistress or their... particular lady..." A blush hit her cheeks but she continued on regardless. "They often bring a gift with them. A valuable gift." Tilting her head, Lady Newfield lifted one shoulder. "At times, if they are bringing the connection to an end, the gentleman will furnish the lady with a most expensive gift. Perhaps a ruby necklace and set of pearls."

"I see." Julianna blinked quickly and looked away, torn between embarrassment and upset. "And you think that my husband was on his way to see his mistress."

"It is a reasonable assumption," Lady Newfield said quietly. "It is not as though gentlemen often go about with expensive gifts with them, not unless they are seeking to betroth themselves to a lady or perhaps to make amends for some wrong done." Pressing her lips together, Lady Newfield held Julianna's gaze, whilst Julianna herself began to nod slowly, to show that she understood. "He was very reluctant to inform us about what the item was, which makes me all the more aware that—"

"That your assumptions are, most likely, correct," Julianna said, trying to speak with a firmness she did not feel. "I quite understand, Grandmama." Her smile was a little sorrowful, touching the corners of her lips. "Thank you for explaining it to me."

Lady Newfield sighed heavily again. "Would that I did not have to," she said with a shake of her head. "I confess, Julianna, I had hoped that in bringing you here, we might be able to find some sort of goodness in your husband—even a small amount which we might then use to our advantage." She shook her head, looking over Julianna's shoulder to where Lord Altringham still stood. "And now I begin to fear that I am quite mistaken."

"It does not matter," Julianna replied, turning and taking her grandmother's arm so that they might walk together. "It is in the past now, is it not? There is nothing I can do. Lord Altringham is my husband, whether I wish him to be or not. Thus, I must try and find even a sliver of goodness within him which can be used to bring him toward me." She gave her grandmother a rueful smile. "Or at least a sense of shame and guilt which might, in turn, do what we wish it."

Unfortunately, Lady Newfield did not smile. "I only wish that you had been blessed with a better husband," she said heavily. "I am aware that to be the wife of an earl is a most excellent connection, but I would have rather seen you wed to a thoughtful, honest, welcoming gentleman instead of one who is so utterly without any sort of kindness."

Julianna nodded but said nothing more. Her heart and mind were full of all manner of thoughts and emotions, but there was something there now that had not been present before. A curiosity, perhaps. An eagerness to discover just what had gone on. She supposed the perpetrator must have jumped out of the other side of the carriage rather than linger, which was why Lord Altringham did not give chase. There was nowhere to go, nowhere to look. It was as though a shadow had entered the carriage and slipped away with this item of great worth—whatever it was.

"You have become very quiet, my dear," Lady Newfield murmured as they began to catch up to Lady Tillsbury and Miss Glover, who had now come to a standstill and were waiting for them. "You are quite all right, I hope?"

Julianna hesitated. "I have some considerations that I would like to give time to," she said honestly. "But for the moment, I am quite well."

Lady Newfield smiled. "Your courage is beginning to blossom, I see," she said, making Julianna glow with contentment at the remark. "I am glad." She pressed Julianna's arm. "Long may it last."

CHAPTER SIX

The theft of what had been a most expensive gift of a diamond pendant and bracelet was, to Thomas' mind, not only worrying but greatly frustrating. He could not quite believe that it was gone, and certainly could not imagine who had done such a thing.

"Gone, you say?" Lord Fairfax murmured as they wandered around Lord Millerford's large drawing room. The music room and library were also filled with guests but he and Lord Fairfax had come in search of brandy—and brandy they had found. "How can that be?"

Thomas let out a long breath. "I do not know," he muttered darkly. "I was alerted to it by Miss Sussex, who was out walking with some acquaintance or other and apparently saw someone making their way into my carriage!"

"And the driver did not notice?" Lord Fairfax asked, frowning hard as Thomas nodded. "You do not think that...?" He trailed off, not finishing his thought, which, in turn, made Thomas' interest all the more piqued.

"Please," he said quickly, looking at his friend in interest. "What is it that you wanted to suggest?"

Again, Lord Fairfax hesitated, then shrugged as though he had considered what Thomas' reaction might be but would think nothing of it regardless.

"What if your driver was bribed so that he would *not* notice?" he asked, making Thomas stop dead as he stared at Lord Fairfax, his stomach suddenly churning in a most uncomfortable manner. "I do not mean to question your staff, of course, but that is something that mayhap you ought to consider."

Thomas let out a long breath, looking nowhere in particular as his mind began to chew over the possibility that his driver and tiger had been given money in order to look the other way when the gift had been stolen.

"No," he said after a few moments. "I do not think such a thing could have been the case."

"No?" Lord Fairfax queried, one eyebrow lifted. "And why do you dismiss the idea so quickly?"

Thomas tried to explain. "Because my driver and my tiger would not have known that I was taking the gift that particular afternoon." He shrugged. "I did not tell the driver my intention to go to Lady Guthrie's after Hyde Park."

This did not seem to satisfy Lord Fairfax, who shook his head firmly. "That does not mean that they were not paid to ignore the intruder. They would have just been told to ignore this person but not been given a specific time as to when they would approach."

Sighing, Thomas let his shoulders drop, rubbing his forehead with one hand. "I do not like the idea of my staff being so easily manipulated," he said begrudgingly. "And I am not about to remove them from their position without further proof."

"That is wise," Lord Fairfax agreed, "particularly given that anyone you might replace your driver with could be easily bribed also."

This remark, however, did not help Thomas in any way. In fact, it left him all the more confused.

"And which of your acquaintances did you inform of your intention to bring such a gift to Lady Guthrie?" Lord Fairfax asked with a sharp look toward Thomas. "That should also be something else you consider. That might, in fact, aid you in finding the person responsible."

At this, Thomas felt his cheeks begin to heat as embarrassment climbed up his spine. "That, I fear, I cannot help you with," he said, a little awkwardly. "I was in White's the previous evening and I may have drunk a little more than I ought to have done."

Rolling his eyes, Lord Fairfax let out his breath heavily. "You mean to say you were in your cups and spoke of your intentions to all who would listen?"

"I did not mean to do so," Thomas protested, as though he were trying to justify himself to a disapproving parent. "But yes, I believe that I was a little too open with those in White's who were about me. I told everyone I intended to bring things to a close with Lady Guthrie along with the fact that I would be giving her a very expensive parting gift the following day."

Lord Fairfax brought his brandy to his lips and took a very large sip. "I see," he muttered, shaking his head. "I do not know what else I can do in order to assist you, Lord Altringham, given that you have told quite a number of gentlemen—including some, I am sure, that you are not even acquainted with—precisely what your intentions were."

"But I did not expect anyone to thereafter come and steal the diamonds from my carriage," Thomas replied, frustrated. "What sort of gentleman does such a thing?"

Lifting his brow, Lord Fairfax spread one hand out. "Gentlemen who are a little short of funds at the present moment?" he suggested. "Gentlemen who have a good many debts and have not yet got the means to pay them? Gentlemen who have a dislike of you and want to cause you difficulty? Gentlemen who bear a grudge for something you have done?" He looked at Thomas pointedly. "And you know full well that there are more than a few of these."

As much as he did not want to either hear or admit to such things, Thomas had to nod and agree that there were many gentlemen who might want to do such a thing in order to bring him difficulty. "I do not know what I ought to do next, however," he said, taking a sip of his brandy. "The diamonds were very expensive and Lady Guthrie still believes our connection to be just as it always was." Gritting his teeth with the sudden rush of frustration that ran over him, Thomas clenched one fist hard. "I wanted to bring that to a swift end and yet now it seems I am going to have to linger with that connection for a short time."

"Until you can purchase *more* diamonds," Lord

Fairfax said with a grin. "Although I am surprised you want to end your time with Lady Guthrie. I thought she was of some importance to you."

Thomas hesitated, wondering how to express his reason to end his association with Lady Guthrie when, in truth, he was not quite certain what it was himself. A vision of Miss Sussex came into his mind and he shook his head in order to clear his thoughts, garnering a puzzled look from Lord Fairfax.

"I do not quite know, to be truthful," he admitted, surprising himself with his willingness to be somewhat vulnerable with Lord Fairfax. "There is something about Lady Guthrie that irritates me, I think. I have not grown tired of her but perhaps realized that she is not the sort of lady I wish to spend my time with."

Lord Fairfax's lips quirked. "Then you hope to replace her with someone else," he said dryly. "Lady Darlington, mayhap?"

About to answer, Thomas' answer dried on his lips as he saw none other than Miss Sussex walking toward him, her head turned toward her companion. A Miss Glover, if he remembered correctly. The way Miss Sussex had been pulled away from him yesterday had brought him a struggle within his heart that he had not particularly enjoyed. It was as if he had wanted her to remain close to him and was saddened by her departure. It was a very odd sensation but he had been unable to rid himself of it either. And now that he saw her again, he wanted nothing more than to go to her and speak to her about what had happened the previous afternoon—indeed, to *thank* her for her willingness to come and speak to him when he had behaved with such indiscretion and coarseness with Miss Darlington at the ball.

"Miss Sussex!"

The way he called her name brought him a bit of attention but Thomas ignored the turned heads and the flickers of interest in the eyes that watched him. Instead, he smiled warmly as Miss Sussex lifted her head and looked at him, a flash of surprise in her eyes. Then, she turned her head back to her friend, who looked at him again, ruefully, and somewhat reluctantly, nodding.

"Pray speak to Miss Glover, Lord Fairfax," Thomas said quickly. "I must have a few words with Miss Sussex without interruption from her fair friend."

Lord Fairfax cleared his throat, handing his empty glass to a footman and then placing his hands behind his back. "But of course," he murmured, sounding quite pleased. "A Miss Glover, did you say?"

There was no time to answer in the affirmative, for Miss Glover and Miss Sussex joined them, curtsying in greeting. Quickly, Thomas introduced Lord Fairfax, who, he noted, was looking with interest at Miss Glover.

"You are recovered after yesterday's incident, then?" Miss Sussex asked, a slight reserve in her manner. She was not looking directly at him, her voice cool and her expression a little muted. Thomas felt himself coloring. It was clear that she had understood precisely who was to be the recipient of the gift of diamonds and obviously, she did not approve. On top of which, she had witnessed him with Lady Darlington and had dealt with the insult of him refusing to dance with her. How little she must think of him!

And why should you care? he asked himself. *You are a rake. Everyone in the beau monde is aware of it and you have never felt such embarrassment before.*

It was not something he could explain and thus, he felt himself rather awkward as he assured her he was quite well and was only disappointed and confused as to the theft of his diamonds.

"I am very sorry for the theft," Miss Sussex replied as Lord Fairfax began to speak to Miss Glover. "I do hope you will be able to find them."

He shook his head. "Unfortunately, I do not think such a thing will be possible," he said with a sigh. "But the diamonds themselves are not of great importance. What troubles me the most is the thought that someone of my acquaintance had decided to steal them from me in the first place."

Miss Sussex looked at him steadily for a few minutes, her light blue eyes fixed to his. It was as though she were assessing him, trying to decipher whether or not his words were the truth. Thomas did not much like the steadiness of her gaze, noting to himself the difference in her from when they had first been introduced. It appeared that she had a trifle more fortitude now, as though she were no longer afraid to look at him with a directness that had been entirely absent before.

"I am sorry I could not be of any more help," Miss Sussex said eventually. "Mayhap if I had come to speak to you a little more urgently, then you might have been able to capture the perpetrator."

An urge to ensure that Miss Sussex herself felt no responsibility began to surge within him and he took a small step forward, seeing her eyes flare as he did so.

"I would not want you to take on any blame in this matter," he said quietly, seeing her cheeks beginning to color. "You did nothing wrong, Miss Sussex. Instead, I ought to be profusely thanking you for what you did." Smiling at her, he waited until the corner of her mouth crept up before continuing. "I am sorry I was rather cool toward you when you first approached. That was my own foolishness and arrogance and there is no excuse for it." It was not often that Thomas apologized and, on occasion, when he had to do so, he found himself to be less than genuine. However, in this case, he found himself truly sincere, recalling how he had turned his head away as Miss Sussex had come to the group. "I am truly sorry, Miss Sussex, and very grateful for your willingness to come and inform me about what you had seen, particularly when I had not treated you with kindness or respect the previous evening."

This seemed to surprise Miss Sussex, for her brows rose and her eyes widened, but in a moment, the expression was gone and she had inclined her head, breaking the connection between them for a second.

"You need not thank me" she said graciously. "I would have done the same for anyone of my acquaintance, of course."

"That is because you have a very good heart, Miss Sussex," he replied honestly. "You are everything that I am not, my dear lady, and that is something I am becoming more and more aware of."

The moment those words left his lips, Thomas felt as though he had taken something hidden from his heart and had revealed it to the entire room. He had not meant to speak with such truth or such vulnerability and yet there had been something about Miss Sussex that had brought it out from within him. She had not expected it either, her eyes wide with surprise, her mouth a perfect circle. Thomas felt his throat go dry, not quite certain what he ought to do or say next. He was a rake, he told himself, and he liked such a title. Was it true that he really wished to change? What was it about Miss Sussex that had him so eager to change how he was at present? His breath came out from him slowly as he looked at her, aware that the silence between them had now brought with it a strong sense of awkwardness.

"I confess I am surprised to hear such a thing from you," Miss Sussex said slowly, looking at him with those wide, astonished eyes. "I thought you were very contented with your life as it is at present."

Thomas opened his mouth to say that yes, he was quite contented, but found that he simply could not say such a thing for he knew it would be something of a lie. After all, that was why he had intended to bring things to an end with Lady Guthrie, was it not? And why he had not sought out Lady Darlington in order to make amends? Were he honest with himself, he had no desire to go to either of them, to be in their company or even in their presence. It was something he could not explain and something that he found very perplexing indeed.

"But if you wish to change your ways, then I can only

encourage you to do so," Miss Sussex continued as she looked at him steadily. "I am sure you would surprise a good many people, however."

"Including myself," he muttered, rubbing his forehead. "Forgive me, Miss Sussex. I do not think I am making particular sense this evening."

She laughed and Thomas' head lifted, his eyes fixed to hers and a small smile touching his mouth. He had never heard her laugh before and the sound was melodious and filled with happiness. It made him smile, seeing how her face was transformed as she laughed. Her eyes sparkled, her smile bright and her whole face lit with good humor. He could not help but smile back at her, finding himself quite captured by the sound. Why had he ever thought of her as plain? She was not plain by any means. Rather, she was quite lovely in her own way.

"I think you are making perfect sense, Lord Altringham," Miss Sussex said, stepping forward and putting one hand on his arm for just a moment. "It may be that you simply do not wish to continue along this new path that your thoughts and intentions are trying to take you."

Her hand lifted and Thomas felt the loss immediately. He wanted to reach out and grasp her hand again, to feel that connection for a moment longer. What astonished him all the more was that he did not have the urge to try and encourage her to come along with him to a quiet part of the room, or to the terrace or another room entirely, so that he might be able to steal a kiss or two from her. This was not a usual reaction from him, for he was always thinking of what he could do in order to convince a lady to go with him for such a thing. He was continually thinking of his own pleasures, except, it seemed, with Miss Sussex. What was it about her that made him behave so? Was it because he had thought her plain? Because he had considered her unworthy of his attentions? And now that he realized just how kind a heart she had, how gentle a spirit was within her, he found himself unwilling to treat her as he did so many others. That was the truth of it, he realized, a cold hand grasping his heart. He did not consider other ladies in the way he considered Miss Sussex. There was nothing of substance between himself and any other lady of his acquaintance. He did not know them. He cared nothing for what they liked or disliked, what they thought of, what they hoped for. All he wanted was their attentions for a short while until, thereafter, he brought the relationship to a close.

"You appear quite contemplative, Lord Altringham."

Starting slightly in surprise, he looked at Miss Sussex and saw the small smile playing about her mouth. "Yes, indeed," he agreed, a little embarrassed. "You seem to bring out the meditative side of me, Miss Sussex."

She laughed again and he could not help but smile. "Perhaps that is not a bad thing, Lord Altringham," she suggested, and he nodded in agreement.

"I do not think it is," he found himself saying. "Might you wish to bring it out from within me again, Miss Sussex?" Seeing her frown, he tried to express himself a little better. "What I mean to say is, would you wish to walk with me tomorrow afternoon? St. James' Park, mayhap?"

Miss Sussex went suddenly still, her eyes fixed to his, her lip caught between her teeth. She was considering his question carefully, he could tell, her hands held tightly together in front of her.

"Lady Newfield would attend with me, of course," she said slowly, looking at him carefully. "You are aware of that, Lord Altringham?"

He nodded, surprised that he did not mind what he would have previously considered to be an unwelcome intrusion. "But of course," he said, spreading his hands. "I would not discourage you from taking your chaperone with you, Miss Sussex. Truly."

She nodded slowly, still considering him for a few moments. And then, much to his relief, she smiled softly.

"I should like that, Lord Altringham," she said demurely. "Tomorrow afternoon, did you say?"

Grinning, he nodded his head. "Shall we say at three o' clock?" he asked, and she smiled her agreement. "I will not be tardy, Miss Sussex."

"What is this?" Miss Glover took a couple of steps toward Miss Sussex, with Lord Fairfax clearing his throat as he came to join them again. "You are not making plans with Lord Altringham, I hope, Miss Sussex?"

Her sharp eyes and dark frown told Thomas that Miss Glover knew precisely the sort of gentleman he was and that she disapproved of him completely.

"I am, Miss Glover," Miss Sussex replied with a firm confidence in her voice. "Lady Newfield will be attending with me also, of course."

Miss Glover rolled her eyes and shot Thomas a hard look. "That is a relief, at least," she said sternly. "And you must not attempt to remove Miss Sussex from her chaperone, Lord Altringham."

He held up one hand in defense. "I give you my word that I will not do so, Miss Glover," he vowed. "Although I am certain that you do not believe my word either."

"For good reason," she snapped back as he gave her a small shrug. "But I must insist that you take good care of my dear friend, Lord Altringham. I shall not be satisfied if you do not."

Miss Sussex pressed her friend's arm. "I am certain that Lord Altringham will do precisely as you have asked," she said, her calm voice smoothing over the palpable tension that was between himself and Miss Glover. "Now, shall we go in search of Lady Newfield to inform her of this?" Her eyes held Miss Glover's, who, after a moment or two, nodded.

"Do excuse us," Miss Sussex murmured, inclining her head. "I look forward to tomorrow, Lord Altringham."

"As do I," he found himself saying, aware that, as he spoke, he meant every single word.

"You look quite lovely this afternoon."

Miss Sussex looked up at Thomas, her face tilting to his. "You are very kind to say so," she answered modestly. "I thank you for your invitation to walk in the park today. The day is very fine and I am glad for the opportunity to step outside."

Thomas smiled and then glanced behind him, where

Lady Newfield walked, albeit only a step or two behind them. She did not smile, looking back at him with a sharpness to her gaze that warned him she watched every single move he made.

"The day is very fine indeed," he answered, finding himself a little awkward when it came to conversation. "I do like St. James' Park."

Miss Sussex said nothing, looking at him and then dropping her gaze back to the path ahead. Thomas found himself struggling to find what he could say next. This was not a situation he was used to and thus, he was beginning to find it grating.

"What is it you are thinking, Lord Altringham?"

Miss Sussex's gentle voice broke into his thoughts and he glanced down at her, seeing how her eyes were on his. "What is it that occupies you?" she asked. "I find you very quiet indeed."

Embarrassment flooded him. "I do not mean to be poor company," he said hastily. "If I am to be honest, I would say that I..." Trailing off, he struggled to find a suitable excuse for his lack of conversation. "I am not..."

"You are unused to having a deep conversation with a lady?" Miss Sussex asked, a small smile creeping onto her face. "Is that what you mean to say?"

A little astonished that she had understood him so, without him even expressing anything of the sort, Thomas stopped dead and looked at her. Behind him, Lady Newfield's footsteps began to slow, letting him know that she was listening also.

"That is precisely what I meant to express," he said

truthfully. "I did not expect you to see such a thing within my conversation."

She laughed and instantly, Thomas felt himself begin to relax, with some of the tension he now felt draining away.

"You are unused to walking and conversing with a lady in such a manner, no?" she asked with a small smile. "You are instead used to stealing a lady's affections and attentions rather than listening to what they have to say and attempting to show a genuine interest," she said, looking at him with a confidence to her manner that surprised him. "But I shall not be upset, Lord Altringham. Rather, I feel myself glad that you have chosen to walk with me this afternoon, rather than attempting to do anything else."

He could not help but chuckle. "You have found the truth of the matter, Miss Sussex," he told her with a small shrug. "I cannot say otherwise."

"As I have said, I am not insulted," she answered. "Instead, I am grateful." Her head turned back toward the path. "What is it you would like to speak of?" She laughed again as he looked at her, a little confused. "There must be *some* topic which you would like to discuss!"

Thomas frowned, trying hard to think of what he could speak of with the lady. "Might you tell me a little more about you?" he asked, seeing that Miss Sussex stiffened slightly at the question, her eyes flaring for a moment before she turned her head away. "I feel as though I do not know you particularly well, Miss Sussex, and I should like to change that."

Pressing her lips together, Miss Sussex looked up at him before turning her head away.

"If you wish to know the sort of person I am, then I can tell you that I do enjoy reading, although I am not a great reader. I enjoy walking out of doors whenever I can and love nothing more than sitting somewhere outside— either here or at home—when I can watch all that occurs." Her face lit up, her eyes taking on a distant view. "I like to hear the birds sing and listen to the wind when it brushes through the trees. I feel quite at home, quite safe, and without any need to hide myself away." Her smile became a little sad. "I am not ignored then. I am merely a part of all that is going on."

Thomas frowned, looking into her face and seeing a mix of sadness and contentment mixed into Miss Sussex's expression. There was more to her than she wanted to say, he realized, his stomach dropping low as he wondered what it was she had kept hidden. What was the cause of her sadness? Why did she speak of hiding, of being ignored? What was it that brought her so much pain?

"Miss Sussex, I—"

Before he could finish his sentence, something slammed hard into his shoulder, throwing him back. Miss Sussex let out a sudden scream of shock and pain began to rifle through him, spreading out from his shoulder and all down his arm. He did not know what had happened to him, did not know what was going on, only to see Miss Sussex press her handkerchief to his shoulder, redness blotting it almost at once.

"What happened?" Lady Newfield cried, bending

down over him beside Miss Sussex. "Are you all right, Julianna?"

Miss Sussex nodded, her expression grim. "I am well," she told her companion. "But Lord Altringham..." She looked at him, her face set. "I believe you have been shot."

CHAPTER SEVEN

J ulianna shuddered as she washed her hands, seeing the final few strands of red swirling into the water and feeling grateful for the small fire burning in the grate. One moment she had been talking to Lord Altringham, and the next he had been thrown back, crashing to the ground. She had seen him press his shoulder and had, to her shock, caught a flash of red on his shirt. On instinct, she had pressed her handkerchief to Lord Altringham's shoulder, even though it had not done a great deal save for confirming that what she had suspected was, in fact, the case.

Lord Altringham had been shot. There was no other explanation for what had occurred. A bullet in his shoulder just above his heart, leaving blood pouring from the wound. Had Lady Newfield not been present, Julianna was not certain what she would have done. Lady Newfield had pressed not only her handkerchief but also Julianna's to the wound, before sending Julianna to go and fetch the carriage as quickly as she could. She had been in so much of a daze that her feet had felt like blocks of wood as she made her way toward the carriage, stumbling slightly as she went. The driver and tiger had come to fetch Lord Altringham at once, and they had all been taken back to his townhouse where she now waited.

Looking at her reflection in the mirror, Julianna saw a pale-cheeked young lady, whose blonde hair was all of a tangle. Her curls had already begun to come undone from all of the commotion, her pins slipping from their place. With a heavy sigh, Julianna began to pull out the pins one at a time, knowing that she would have to set her hair back in place herself. It was not something she was unused to, given that she had been made to fix her own hair on many an occasion whilst under her father's roof. He did not care for fripperies and apparently allowing a maid to do her hair, other than on the night of a ball or some such thing, was entirely unnecessary and would take the maid away from her work.

Running her fingers through her hair, Julianna let out a long breath, trying to steady herself. She had been shivering with shock as she had been welcomed into the house, and the butler had encouraged her into this small room where she could wash her hands and warm herself by the fire if she wished to for a short time. Lady Newfield was waiting for her in the drawing room and the doctor was with Lord Altringham. She had a few moments to collect herself.

The door to her left suddenly opened and Lord Altringham staggered in. He was in his shirtsleeves, blood still staining the shoulder and the arm of his shirt, and his feet were bare.

Julianna gasped in shock and stepped back, not quite sure where to look.

Lord Altringham blinked and then cleared his throat. "My apologies," he said bluntly. "I did not think anyone was in here."

"I apologize," Julianna murmured, not looking at him but rather turning a little to her left. "If you need something from within, I shall, of course, leave at once."

Lord Altringham waved a hand, his eyes fixed on her long, fair hair which was now curling around her shoulders and back. "No, it is of no importance," he said firmly. "I thought there might be a fire in here and intended to simply throw my shirt on it." He shrugged. "It is quite ruined."

Heat burned in her face as she turned herself away. "I would not prevent you," she said, gesturing to the fire. "Only please do excuse me first, Lord Altringham." A sudden thought had her looking at him sharply. "I do hope that this is not an attempt to..." She could not bring herself to finish speaking, suddenly horrified at the thought that he might be trying to encourage her into his arms.

His reaction was one of anger.

"No, Miss Sussex," he said furiously, his eyes boring into hers. "No, I am not attempting to seduce you. I merely came to throw my shirt on the fire. That is all. I had no awareness that you were present in this room." He gestured toward the door. "Please, take your leave. I should not want to embarrass you further or make you think any worse of me."

Julianna hurried out of the room at once, her eyes

burning with unshed tears. She had somehow managed to insult him without having had any intention of doing so. She had been caught by surprise and had jumped to the worst conclusion. It had been foolish of her now, she realized, dragging air into her tight lungs as she made her way to the drawing room, which she had been shown to at the first before being taken to the room to wash her hands and refresh herself.

"Goodness, Julianna!" Lady Newfield exclaimed as Julianna walked inside. "What on earth has occurred?" Her eyes flared as she grasped Julianna by the shoulders. "Lord Altringham has not...?"

Julianna closed her eyes and shook her head. "No, he has done nothing," she said, realizing that her grandmother was talking about her hair. "My hair was coming undone and I intended to put it all back up before I returned to you, but Lord Altringham surprised me and I had to quit the room quickly."

Lady Newfield blinked, trying clearly to make sense of what Julianna had said. "You mean, you had to escape him?"

Opening her eyes, Julianna took in a deep breath and tried to explain. "No, Grandmama," she said softly. "I insulted him and had to take my leave quickly." She swallowed hard and prayed that no tears would come to her eyes. "I think it would be best if we left at once."

"We cannot leave immediately," Lady Newfield said slowly. "Not when your hair is in such a state." Taking Julianna's hand, she led her to the couch and sat down beside her. "Do hurry now."

Together, both Julianna and Lady Newfield quickly

managed to get Julianna's hair up into a very sensible chignon and, given that there were no interruptions, felt quite able to then depart. Rising to her feet, Julianna let out a long breath and made for the door, only for it to open before she could reach it.

"Lady Newfield, Miss Sussex." Lord Altringham came into the room, making Julianna stop dead. "You were not leaving, I hope? I have had refreshments sent for and they will be here momentarily."

Julianna glanced behind her to Lady Newfield, who had pasted a smile on her face although her eyes remained steady.

"We can only stay for a short while, Lord Altringham," she said smoothly, "just to ensure you are a little recovered."

Lord Altringham returned Lady Newfield's smile but did not look at Julianna. "I am quite well, I assure you," he said, gesturing to his shoulder. "An injury here, yes, but aside from that, I feel very well indeed." Coming a little further into the room, he gestured to the chairs and couches. "Please, do sit and take tea with me. I would be most grateful, especially after what you have done."

"I do not think we did a great deal," Lady Newfield said, but she moved to sit down regardless, leaving Julianna to follow. "All that matters is that you are not gravely injured."

Lord Altringham's face twisted as the door opened to reveal two maids bringing in trays of refreshments. He did not speak until they had left, his expression still dark. "I am sure that someone *did* wish to gravely injure me," he said, his tone somber. "I am aware of just how close to my heart that bullet came."

Julianna's heart quickened as she saw the flicker of fear in Lord Altringham's eyes. "Do you think the same person who stole your diamonds also did this?" she asked, and Lord Altringham looked at her for the first time since he had entered the room. "It seems quite an escalation to go from the theft of diamonds to shooting you."

Lord Altringham rubbed his chin, his eyes dropping to the floor as he considered what she had suggested.

"That is quite true, Miss Sussex," Lady Newfield said slowly. "To go from stealing to attempting to murder someone does seem to be two very separate incidents with two separate motivations."

"One to steal from you for their own gains and for your shame, with the other seemingly to steal your life from you," Julianna murmured, looking at Lord Altringham and noting him a little paler. "Could it be that there are two separate people attempting to injure you in their own ways?"

Lord Altringham let out a long breath. "Mayhap," he said quietly. "You might very well speak the truth, Miss Sussex, but I cannot say for certain. However, I must confess that I am now much more on my guard."

Lady Newfield gestured to the tea tray, catching Julianna's eye as she did so. A little embarrassed, Julianna glanced at Lord Altringham. "Might I—might I pour the tea, Lord Altringham?" she asked, seeing his eyes flare as though he had forgotten all about the refreshments that had been brought in.

"Yes, yes, of course," he said quickly, gesturing toward her. "Please, Miss Sussex."

She did so at once, glad that her hands did not tremble as she lifted the teapot. Soon, they all had a cup of tea and a cake or two to hand, with the first sip of Julianna's tea tasting more refreshing than ever before. Even Lord Altringham seemed to relax a little as he lifted the cup to his mouth.

"It seems a little foolish to ask who might have something against you, Lord Altringham," Lady Newfield said, her eyes firm as she spoke bluntly, making Julianna gasp in shock. "For I presume there will be a quite a few gentlemen who see you as nothing more than a rake who deserves every manner of punishment."

Setting her tea down, Julianna clasped her hands tightly, her body rigid with tension as she looked at Lord Altringham, expecting him to retort angrily at her grandmother.

Instead, he merely sighed and spread his hands. "You are quite correct, Lady Newfield," he said without any attempt to put himself in a better light. "There are a few. I am a rake and thus, have treated a good many gentlemen without any consideration when I have sought out the ladies that please me." Sighing, he dropped his head low. "I have no one to blame but myself," he added. "I have found myself wanting to turn away from this path these last few days, without any explanation as to why..." He glanced up at Julianna for a moment, who felt a thrill of heat climb up her spine at his mere glance. "And I suppose that this is the confirmation that is required for me to make that change permanent."

Something like joy shot up from Julianna's core and it took all of her efforts to keep her face composed. Could this be true? Could Lord Altringham truly change his character? Did that mean that she could have hope that one day, he might become the sort of husband she needed him to be?

But what will he say when he discovers you have been lying to him about who you are? came a quiet voice in her heart. *What will he say then?*

"You must be careful," Lady Newfield cautioned, looking at Lord Altringham with a curiosity in her gaze, as though she were uncertain as to whether or not to believe him. "Someone is clearly desperate to remove you from this earth."

"And I cannot even begin to imagine who it could be, since there are so many who wish me ill," Lord Altringham said gloomily. "What is it I am to do?" He looked from Julianna to Lady Newfield as though he needed them to give him some answers, some explanations as to what was required. "I do not know. Should I remain at home? Hiding away?" He glanced at Julianna as he said this, the word 'hiding' reminding her of what she herself had said to him earlier that day. That had been when she had, mayhap, spoken a little too freely and with a little less care. Somewhat embarrassed, she hid her feelings by picking up her teacup and taking another sip.

"I do not think that it is wise for you to hide yourself here, Lord Altringham, no," Lady Newfield said slowly. "But at the same time, you must be wise in your choice of outings."

"Balls, for example, would be quite all right, would they not?" Julianna chimed in, quickly understanding what her grandmother meant. "With so many people, no one would dare attempt to shoot you."

Lord Altringham chuckled somewhat wryly. "No, I suppose they would not."

"Although you would need to be careful not to go into the gardens or any more secretive places," Lady Newfield finished, one eyebrow arching. "But that, I would think, would fit into your newfound attempt to improve your behavior, would it not?"

Again, Lord Altringham chuckled, rubbing one hand over his forehead. "It would indeed, Lady Newfield," he said with a shake of his head. His expression suddenly became serious as he glanced from Julianna to Lady Newfield and back again. "I will not pretend that it is not a little worrying to have had someone almost succeeding to put a bullet through my heart," he added, his brows now so low that they almost knotted together. "And there are so few of my acquaintances to whom I can give my trust that I—"

"There must be someone," Julianna interrupted, speaking softly. "Surely one of your acquaintances is trustworthy."

Lord Altringham hesitated, then nodded slowly. "Yes, there is Lord Fairfax," he said, and Julianna remembered the gentleman that Miss Glover had spoken to while she was speaking to Lord Altringham at the evening soiree. "He is one of my only true friends and has no hesitation in telling me when he believes me to have overstepped."

Julianna was a little surprised to hear that such a gentleman would be a friend of Lord Altringham's when, evidently, they were so different—knowing little of Lord Fairfax's character—yet she was grateful that he had someone upon whom he could rely.

"And, of course, I have you, Miss Sussex."

Turning her eyes back toward him, Julianna felt her stomach tighten at the look in his eyes.

"I am sorry about before," he said plainly. "I reacted badly to what was a very fair assumption on your part. Forgive me."

She shook her head wordlessly, trying to find the words to protest, but Lord Altringham held up one hand.

"Please, no words to try and attribute some blame to your own actions, Miss Sussex," he said firmly. "I will not hear of it. I am sorry for behaving so, especially after all you have done to help me. Forgive me, please."

Seeing the astonishment on Lady Newfield's face, Julianna found herself smiling. "But of course, Lord Altringham," she said quietly. "And you are quite correct, you do have both myself and Lady Newfield by you. Neither of us have any desire to harm you and will be as much help to you as we can be."

Lord Altringham let out a long, slow breath, turning his head a little so that he might rub the back of his neck in evident frustration.

"I feel as though I have stepped into another life," he said, as though speaking to himself. "One where I must be on my guard and wary of all those around me." Sighing, he winced and looked back at Julianna. "My sins have caught up with me now, it seems. The consequences of my behavior have finally come to rest heavily upon my shoulders." His eyes were bleak. "I do not know which one of my acquaintances bears an outward appearance of joviality but inwardly has an entirely different intention for me."

Julianna wanted to say that he did not deserve to have his life stolen from him, no matter what he had done, but found that his last sentence seemed to have pulled her breath from her. Was she not as he had stated? Outwardly, pretending to be Miss Sussex, chaperoned by a family friend, whilst inwardly knowing that she was, in fact, his wife and thus having an entirely different intention as regards her acquaintance with him? Her lungs were burning, her head buzzing, but as she looked at Lady Newfield, she saw her grandmother give her the tiniest shake of her head as though she knew what Julianna was thinking and was warning her against saying anything.

"We should take our leave now and let you rest," Lady Newfield said firmly, rising from her chair and coming to stand by Julianna, who hastily got to her feet, her tea cooling and forgotten in her cup. "When do you next intend to step out into society?"

Lord Altringham rose also and frowned. "I believe I am to attend Lady Marroway's ball tomorrow evening," he said, looking at Julianna keenly. "Will you also be in attendance, Miss Sussex?"

She nodded. "Yes, I believe so," she answered, still feeling a myriad of confusion over what she had heard from Lord Altringham and all that she now felt. "I would be glad to speak to you there."

He looked so relieved that she could not help but smile. "I would be most grateful for your company," he told her, making a small glow begin to burn in her heart. "After all, Miss Sussex, it seems as though you have saved me twice from the danger that would have befallen me."

Shaking her head, Julianna did not accept such an accolade. "I hardly think so, Lord Altringham."

"Regardless," he said firmly, "I am sure I will be a good deal more at ease in your company tomorrow, Miss Sussex, than I would be on my own."

Finding herself rather warmed by this remark, Julianna quickly took her leave, wished him well, and hurried out after her grandmother, feeling herself both conflicted and delighted in equal measure.

"I could tell that you were considering speaking to Lord Altringham about the truth of your identity, Julianna," Lady Newfield said sternly. "I am sorry to have interrupted your intentions, but I cannot in good conscience allow you to do so."

"Why ever not?" Julianna asked as they walked along the street together, with Lady Newfield's arm linked through hers. "Is there something wrong?"

Lady Newfield hesitated, looking at her for a moment before turning her face back to the pavement. "Because Lord Altringham might not be as genuine as he appears," she said carefully. "He may very well be eager in his intentions at present, but if a pretty young lady were to cross his path, bat her eyelashes at him, and offer him something he might very much like to accept, then he may find his resolve rather weakened."

Julianna let out a sigh, realizing that her grandmother

was correct and yet finding a desire still within her to tell Lord Altringham the truth. "I must hope that he is more aware of himself than that."

"Then allow him to *prove* it," Lady Newfield said gently. "And then speak to him of your true identity if you wish. I fear that if you tell him now, you will arouse his anger and his distrust. However, if he proves himself to be determined and decisive in his new way of conducting himself, then I would hope that you might gain a little more understanding from him in that quarter." She smiled at Julianna, who could not help but admit that she understood the point her grandmother was making. "A gentleman who has thought to turn his back on past behavior only to succumb to it again will not be inclined to listen to the reasons for your secrecy. Whereas a gentleman who is aware of his behavior and now considers it to be abhorrent and something to regret will be much more inclined to listen and understand."

"That makes sense, Grandmama," Julianna answered heavily. "Although I must hope that someone does not succeed in their attempt to kill him before that time comes!" She winced. "Not that I wish him dead at all."

Lady Newfield linked her arm through Julianna's. "You need not worry, my dear," she said encouragingly. "It may be that, in this disastrous and difficult situation, both you and Lord Altringham will find yourselves moving toward each other all the more, to the point where he will be delighted and relieved to learn that you are, in fact, his wife." She squeezed Julianna's arm lightly. "And you yourself have developed in courage, strength, and determination, my dear, and that has been quite wonderful to see."

"Thank you, Grandmama," Julianna murmured as they came to Lady Newfield's townhouse. "Let us just hope that Lord Altringham thinks it to be just as wonderful when he discovers the truth."

CHAPTER EIGHT

T he ball was in full swing by the time Thomas arrived. He had decided to linger at home for a little longer than usual, telling himself that he was being wise rather than afraid of what might be waiting for him.

Stepping inside, having greeted his hostess, Thomas looked out across the room and felt his stomach tighten. Was there someone here eager to take his life? Someone here who was disappointed to see him standing with the best of the *beau monde*, disappointed that the bullet had not found its way into his heart?

Suppressing a shudder, Thomas walked into the crowd of guests, telling himself that there was no need for him to be afraid in such a setting. It was as Miss Sussex had said. No one would attempt to steal his life from him here in such a public setting, for fear of being seen and caught.

Clearing his throat, he stepped forward and set his shoulders, trying his best to be just as calm and as collected as usual. There were the usual ladies smiling at him and batting their eyelashes, but tonight was the first time he did not find himself reacting to them in the same way. Instead of feeling a flush of delight, he found himself barely able to return their smiles, wondering instead if their posturing hid a snare. Were any of them responsible for the theft of his diamonds? Or capable of shooting a pistol?

"You look a little tense this evening, Altringham."

Thomas stumbled as someone caught his arm. He whirled around on instinct, his hands raised for fear that someone would attack him, only to see Lord Fairfax frowning hard at him.

"Fairfax," he breathed hoarsely. "It is you."

"Yes," Lord Fairfax said slowly, dragging the word out and looking at Thomas with a good deal of concern. "It is only me. Were you expecting someone else?" His eyes narrowed as he saw the way Thomas had his hands raised, making him realize that he was still standing defensively.

"My apologies," Thomas muttered, running one hand through his hair and then immediately regretting doing so, given that he had now mussed it. "You are quite right. I am a little... tense this evening."

Lord Fairfax raised his eyebrows. "And is that for any particular reason?"

Hesitating, Thomas considered whether or not to give him a truthful answer. "I... I have had a few difficulties of late, as you know, what with the diamonds going missing and my struggle to determine whether or not my staff are involved in any way."

"I see," Lord Fairfax murmured thoughtfully. "That

is unfortunate. You have not found out anything about your driver?"

Thomas, who had completely forgotten about questioning his driver as to whether or not he had been involved with the robbery in any way, merely shook his head, choosing not to express this.

"And the diamonds are gone? They have not been found by anyone?"

"No," Thomas said with a sigh. "And Lady Guthrie still does not have them which means that she and I are still, as far as she is concerned, in an agreeable situation."

Lord Fairfax chuckled. "Then mayhap you should simply buy her some rubies and bring things to a close. Rubies are just as good as diamonds."

Thomas snorted. "Not to Lady Guthrie. Diamonds are all she wants." He sighed heavily and rolled his eyes. "But you are quite correct. I should find a way to bring things to a close."

Lord Fairfax looked at him carefully, tilting his head just a little. "Are you quite certain you want to bring things to an end with Lady Guthrie?" he asked quietly. "I know it is not my business, but I did wonder whether or not this has something to do with your marriage."

It was as though Thomas had stepped into an icy river and let the water wash over him. His marriage. He had almost entirely forgotten about these last few days, desperate to put it from his mind and forget about his bride. And he had been so successful in his endeavors that he had, in fact, managed to push all thoughts of her from his mind. He had not even thought of his bride, for his mind had been filled with the confusion of what had been occurring as well as his very odd feeling as regarded Miss Sussex. Just what was he doing? He could have no feelings for Miss Sussex, no considerations for her, nor could he even think of what might be in his heart should he continue his acquaintance, for he was wed now and had a wife of his own already.

But I could always...

Turning a little away from Lord Fairfax, Thomas shook his head. He knew full well that he could not ask Miss Sussex to join him in anything inappropriate. She was not a lady who would be willing to do such a thing, besides which, he did not think that he would even consider asking her. Miss Sussex was not that sort of lady and he, he reminded himself, no longer wanted to be that sort of gentleman.

"You are acting *very* strangely tonight, Lord Altringham, I must say," Lord Fairfax remarked loudly as Thomas swung back toward him. "You are sure there is nothing other than your diamonds and Lady Guthrie?"

"A little quieter, if you please," Thomas hissed, not wanting the rest of the *ton* to overheard Lord Fairfax's remarks. "If you insist on knowing, then I will tell you." Taking a deep breath, he told Lord Fairfax what had happened with the attempt on his life, seeing his friend's eyes widen.

"Gracious," Lord Fairfax murmured, his face a little paler than before. "That is very troubling indeed. Little wonder you are so distracted this evening." His eyes turned to something—or someone—over Thomas' shoulder. "Now, I can see some very lovely distractions coming toward you, Altringham. I'm sure that if you let your mind fill with them, you will soon be turned from your melancholy and distressing thoughts."

Turning, Thomas found himself smiling at Lady Darlington, Miss Marchmont, and Miss Basford, who were all smiling back at him, their eyes warm and their cheeks a little pink from the warmth of the ball. Thomas let out a long breath. Lord Fairfax might be quite correct, Thomas considered, hearing Lord Fairfax letting out a quiet chuckle as Thomas began to greet the ladies, knowing that he would be able to secure two dances from them each. That certainly would distract him from his thoughts for most of the evening!

"You do not want to take a walk with me?"

Lady Darlington looked up at him beseechingly, her eyes like warm honey as she shot him a quick but enticing smile. "It is only a short walk into the gardens," she purred, one hand now tight on his arm, pulling him closer to her. "There are a good many hiding places where we might go, for even a few minutes."

Thomas winced inwardly, feeling the urgent desire to do precisely as she asked, to do *all* that she wished, and knowing that the only reason he was choosing not to do so was simply because of his promise to Miss Sussex. He had told her that he wanted to be a very different gentleman, to turn his back on what he had done before, realizing that the consequences of his prior behavior were now coming back to hit him hard, but now that he was in the moment, standing by Lady Darlington and looking down into her beautiful eyes, he found himself less than eager to do as he had promised. Instead, he wanted to walk out into the gardens with her, to find a quiet place and steal some kisses from her.

"You cannot tell me that you are reluctant to do so *again!*" Lady Darlington huffed, now looking a little petulant. "Whatever is the matter, Lord Altringham? Is it that you no longer wish to accept my attentions?"

"No, no indeed," he found himself saying with such fervor that Lady Darlington's eyes lit up almost at once, her pouting lips curving into a smile. "You must understand, I have promised dances to other young ladies and—"

"You have time," she said, her hands wrapped around his arm as she began to walk toward the door that led to the gardens. "And besides which, am I not more important than a silly dance or two?"

He cleared his throat, feeling himself growing more and more uncomfortable with every step he took. "Yes, of course you are," he said, trying to speak as warmly as he could. "But still, I should not like to upset any of the other ladies I am promised to."

Lady Darlington laughed and patted his arm. "We shall be *very* quick indeed," she smiled, leaning into him all the more. "But I promise you, you will not regret spending a little bit of time with me."

It was a very strange sensation to feel oneself battling between what one wanted to do and what one knew he ought to do, Thomas considered as he was led out of the ballroom by Lady Darlington. There was so much that she had to offer him but the pleasure would be only fleeting, only temporary. He winced as Lady Darlington laughed and pressed his arm again, feeling the pain in his shoulder and recalling, with cold, hard clarity, precisely why he was *not* to step out of the ballroom.

But it was by now much too late. The door was behind him, the darkness already swallowing both himself and Lady Darlington up.

"Wait."

Lady Darlington turned her face to his, staring at him as he stood there, frozen. Her face was flickering in the shadows of the lanterns that had been hung along the garden path and he could see both the astonishment and the impatience in her eyes.

"I am sorry, Lady Darlington," he said, stammering. "I— "

Lady Darlington tossed her head, threw up her hands, and spun on her heel. "I am being spurned again, it seems!" she exclaimed, drawing attention from the other guests. "Good gracious, Lord Altringham, what is it I must do for you to remain with me a little longer?"

Thomas found himself taking a few steps forward, thinking to go after her, only to force himself to come to a stop. There was no need to go after her now, not when he had already made his decision. Yes, she would be upset with him but he could not continue giving in to what she offered, not when he had resolved to change his ways.

Sighing, he turned around and meandered back slowly along the path toward the ballroom. The music no longer seemed to swirl around the air, filled with joy and happiness. The laughter of the guests burned his skin, making him wince as he closed his eyes tightly for a moment. What was happening to him? It was all very strange indeed and he was not at all certain what he was feeling, what was going on within him, and what he ought to do next.

Something hard hit him on the side of the head. He fell sideways, grunting as he did so. Someone was standing near him, and Thomas lifted his hand hopelessly toward his head as a dark figure, clothed in shadow, leaned over him.

"You are unworthy." It was a hiss, a whisper, a breath on the wind. And then it was gone.

And then, a scream rent the air. The shadow was gone and Thomas groaned aloud again, unable to even stand. His head was throbbing and he could feel something warm trickle down the side of his face. What had happened to him?

"Lord Altringham! Lord Altringham!" Lady Darlington exclaimed, having evidently seen what had happened, her voice almost a scream as she leaned over him. "Are you all right?"

He groaned again and tried to push himself up. Lady Darlington stumbled back as some others came near him.

"Get a footman or two," someone commanded. "Whatever happened to you, Lord Altringham?"

"I do not know," Thomas muttered, his head aching all the more as he tried to stand. He felt himself swaying terribly and was grateful for the gentlemen who came to stand by him, helping him to stay upright.

"You are bleeding terribly," said another gentleman, his voice low. "Here." He handed him a kerchief, which Thomas attempted to press against his head, only to wince as the pain in his head doubled. "Did you fall against something?"

Thomas tried to shake his head but gritted his teeth in pain. "No, I did not," he said tightly. "I was struck."

"By what?"

"By whom?" someone else asked, but Thomas could not answer, his head buzzing furiously.

"Good gracious! Is that Altringham?"

Hearing a familiar voice, Thomas tried to make out Lord Fairfax's face in the shadows. Footmen had come to him now, helping him along the pathway.

"I am quite all right," Thomas tried to say, but the words just came out as a mumble. He did not know where he was being led, could not say who was still with him or whether or not Lord Fairfax was with him also. Strong arms helped him climb some steps but no bright lights of the ballroom greeted him. Murmurs and whispers seemed to surround him as he was led into the house, with a door opened in front of him. Struggling to focus, Thomas was put into a soft chair, his head resting back against it.

"I will fetch the apothecary," someone said, and Thomas tried to protest, to say that he did not need such a thing, but his mouth would not work in the way he wished it. Giving in to the pain and the darkness, he closed his eyes and let another groan issue from his mouth. And then he did not feel anything for what felt like a very long time indeed.

❧

"Lord Altringham?"

The sound of a familiar voice prodded Thomas into consciousness. Someone was touching his hand, squeezing his fingers, with something cool pressed against his temple. With an almighty effort, he forced his eyes open, only to have them close again. Struggling hard, he tried to open his eyes again and this time, succeeded in doing so.

Miss Sussex was looking directly into his face, her features fuzzy to his eyes for a short time. He tried to speak but his throat felt like gravel, hoarse and scraping.

"Lord Altringham, you have awakened. Thank goodness," Miss Sussex breathed, grasping his hand a little more tightly. "How do you feel?"

He tried to sit up, only to slump back. He was lying flat on a couch, it seemed, even though he had no recollection of being in such a position.

"Please, do not rush yourself," came another voice. "You have been taken to my townhouse, Lord Altringham. After what happened this evening, we thought it best to take you here."

"Lord Fairfax accompanied us and helped you both in and out of the carriage," Miss Sussex said, letting go of his hand and helping him to sit up, her arm around his shoulders. Thomas let out a groan as his head began to thump with pain, his vision swirling all over again.

"Your head is paining you again," Miss Sussex murmured. "Mayhap I should keep you lying down." With an effort, Thomas managed to grunt his disapproval, wanting to sit up so that he could look all about him. It took all his energy to remain seated and open his eyes again, but he was determined not to lie back down again. Finally, after a few minutes, everything became clear.

Miss Sussex was looking at him with concern, whilst Lady Newfield sat a short distance away, her eyes thoughtful but her lips pulled tight. He did not recognize the room, for the furnishings were entirely different from his drawing room at home.

"Did you say," he managed, his throat still dry and his voice rasping, "that I am in your home, Lady Newfield?"

She nodded, as though this was something that he ought to have expected.

"But why?"

"Because another attempt was made to either injure or kill you!" Miss Sussex exclaimed. "Lord Fairfax said that he did not know what had happened to you, for he only came across you quite by accident when he left the ballroom for a short walk out of doors." Miss Sussex touched his hand again. "You have had a severe blow to the head, Lord Altringham. Had you not been found, you might now be lying in the gardens with your life slowly draining away." Her voice grew quieter with each word that she spoke, her eyes wide with fright. Were Thomas honest, he would admit that her words had confused and frightened him, for he realized that what she said could very well have been the case.

He sucked in a breath, horrified as he recalled how a figure had stood over him, threatening and dark with malevolence.

"He said something," he whispered, closing his eyes in an effort to recall. "I am sure he said something to me."

"Can you remember what it was?" Lady Newfield said quickly as Thomas opened his eyes. "It might give us a hint as to who the perpetrator could be."

Thomas sighed heavily, shaking his head and then instantly regretting that he had done so. The cool cloth that had laid on his forehead as he reclined had fallen to his lap and he lifted it again quickly, pressing it to his aching temple.

"It may come back to you," Miss Sussex said kindly. "You need to rest, Lord Altringham. Do you think you can rise and walk to your room? I can have a footman assist you."

He did not want to admit that he needed assistance but found himself with no other choice.

"I think that would be wise," he said quietly. "Although I do not think that it is required for me to stay any longer than one night."

Lady Newfield cleared her throat, shooting Miss Sussex a knowing look. "We shall discuss matters in the morning," she said firmly. "Now, retire and rest, Lord Altringham. Things will be a good deal clearer tomorrow. Of that, I am quite certain."

CHAPTER NINE

Julianna had thought her desire to tell Lord Altringham the truth to be a good thing, but now that she was faced with it, she felt rather afraid. She did not know how he would react, but given all that had occurred, both she and her grandmother had come to the conclusion that honesty was now required.

"If you continue to pace like that, you will wear yourself out, Julianna," Lady Newfield chided her gently. "Please, do sit down."

Julianna shook her head. "I cannot," she said, twisting her fingers together as she looked back at her grandmother. "I am afraid that he will think me cruel and manipulative and now I..."

Lady Newfield sighed but held Julianna's gaze steadily. "You are not a manipulative creature," she assured her. "And if it should come to it, I shall make quite certain that Lord Altringham knows that it was I who came up with this idea."

"No, Grandmama," Julianna replied quickly. "I will

not have that. After all, you were the one who encouraged me to find courage and strength, and that is what I have tried to do." She lifted her chin, swallowing hard and doing her best to ignore her swirling stomach. "I agreed to this plan, I agreed to do as you thought best and I confess that I believe the scheme has been successful." She gave her grandmother a tight smile. "I do not think that to push the blame onto you would be either wise or honest."

Lady Newfield's smile became warm. There was a pride in her voice as she spoke, which, in turn, filled Julianna with a sense of contentment.

"You have done very well, Julianna," Lady Newfield said, getting to her feet and coming to embrace Julianna. "No matter what happens next, you should be pleased with the steps you have taken and the changes you have made." She reached up and pressed her hand to Julianna's face. "I am very proud of you, my dear girl."

Julianna smiled back at her grandmother, feeling tears coming to her eyes. Had it not been for Lady Newfield, Julianna doubted that she would be where she was at present. Most likely, she would still be under her father's rule, scared and afraid and still ignored by society. Either that or she would be living in Lord Altringham's estate, alone and terrified.

"Good morning."

Lady Newfield stood back from Julianna as the door opened and Lord Altringham walked in. He appeared rather awkward, Julianna noted as she dropped into a quick curtsy. He was looking all about the room, his hands held behind his back and his shoulders tense. Clearing his throat, he shuffled his feet.

"I think I should return to—"

"Do come and sit down and join us for breakfast," Lady Newfield interrupted, gesturing to the dining room table. "We have not eaten either as yet." She gave Julianna a quick glance and Julianna hurried toward the table, sitting down quickly. Lord Altringham finally came to sit down also, feeling, perhaps, as though he could do nothing other than obey Lady Newfield.

"Please, do help yourself," Lady Newfield said encouragingly. "You must eat in order to keep up your strength." She looked pointedly at Lord Altringham's head. "Does your head still pain you?"

Julianna, who had not had a proper look at Lord Altringham's temple, turned her attention to his head also and then caught her breath. There was a dark purple stain spreading out from the side of Lord Altringham's head, looking angry and sore.

"It does not look particularly good, does it?" he said, a little wryly as Julianna's eyes flared wide with the shock of what she had seen. "I will not pretend it does not pain me for I do not think that you would believe me even if I said such a thing!"

"Did you manage to rest at all?" Julianna asked, looking across at him just as Lady Newfield rose from the table to go and fill her plate. "I hope the pain did not keep you awake."

Lord Altringham smiled thinly. "I had a *little* sleep," he said with a shrug of his shoulders. "But I believe that it was not only my head that kept me awake but also the fact that I was considering who might have done such a thing and why they would do it." He sighed, which told Julianna that his questions remained unanswered. "In addition, I was attempting to recall what had been whispered to me by the man who stood over me after his first attempt to bring me low." Lord Altringham's lips twisted and he shook his head. "Unfortunately, I was not successful."

"You are exhausted," Julianna replied gently. "I do not think you should berate yourself for what you cannot remember. It *will* return to you, I am sure."

Lord Altringham held her gaze for a moment and then let out a long sigh. "I must hope that you are correct, Miss Sussex," he said, the name he called her suddenly jarring. "I feel as though, if I were to recall those words, I might be able to determine who it was that has tried to injure me."

"My lady?"

The butler stepped into the room, looking at Lady Newfield and inclining his head. "Forgive the interruption, but you have a visitor."

Lady Newfield's eyes widened in surprise. "This early in the morning?"

The butler cleared his throat, nodding. "Lady Tillsbury wishes to speak to you with the greatest urgency."

Julianna half rose from the table as Lady Newfield caught her breath, before hurrying out toward the door. She herself hesitated, not quite certain whether or not she ought to go with Lady Newfield or remain with Lord Altringham.

"You need not fear remaining here with me," Lord

Altringham said with a rueful smile. "I will not attempt anything, Miss Sussex, I assure you." He raked one hand through his hair, the brown locks rushing through his fingers. "Indeed, after last evening, I find that my resolution to behave in a very different manner than before is now, in fact, quite firm within me."

Julianna did not understand. "What do you mean? That the injury to your head has—"

"I was invited out to the gardens last evening," Lord Altringham interrupted with a tiny smile in Julianna's direction. "I confess that I struggled to know what I ought to do, whether or not I ought to do as the lady asked." Dropping his hands to his lap, he gave another long sigh, his eyes gleaming with what appeared to be regret. "My eagerness to go with her, to do as I usually did, won out over my resolve to change the way in which I behave. However," he continued quickly, as though he wanted to ensure Julianna did not think too poorly of him, "once I was out in the gardens, I realized that I did not want to be where I was. I had to tell the lady in question this and she was, I confess, very angry with me."

Julianna's brows lifted in surprise. "You did not go with her, then?"

"I did not," Lord Altringham answered softly, his eyes fixed to hers and filled with so much feeling that Julianna did not know where to look, wanting to tug her gaze away from him but, at the same time, finding herself quite unable to do so.

"Then I am glad," she found herself saying, filled with such relief that he had not given in to his initial desire. "I am glad for you if you are happy with your choice."

Lord Altringham smiled. "I did not think I would be, but yes, I am very contented indeed. I thought I would be filled with regret, but I confess, there is something within me now that is very proud indeed that I have managed to change."

"I can understand such a feeling," Julianna replied honestly. "Although I am sorry that, despite your choice and your wisdom, you were then so badly attacked."

Reaching up to touch his temple with gentle fingers, Lord Altringham gave her a small, wry smile. "Indeed," he answered with a shrug. "Although, Miss Sussex, I think that I should not remain here for any great length of time. One evening is more than enough."

Her heart began to quicken as she looked into his face, feeling the questions begin to rise up within her, wondering if she ought to ask him why and feeling the urge to tell him the truth of her identity.

"You need not leave," she said softly, putting her hands in her lap so that she could tighten her fingers together in an attempt to keep herself steady. "The reason we insisted that you were brought here is that you might be kept secure. We trust our staff."

Something flickered across Lord Altringham's face.

"It is not to say that your staff are not trustworthy," Julianna said hastily, wondering if she had misspoken. "What I mean to say is that you would be there alone and vulnerable and if you were unconscious, then there is nothing to say that you could not have been attacked again."

Lord Altringham rubbed his hand across his forehead, another long breath escaping him. "I suppose that is true," he said heavily. "I have not yet questioned my staff as to the theft of my diamonds, and I am suspicious that one, if not more, were involved in the theft in some way." Dropping his hand, he looked back at Julianna again. "The truth is, Miss Sussex, I am a little afraid for your reputation."

A cold hand grasped her heart. What was it that Lord Altringham was intending?

"What I mean by that," he continued quickly, as though he wanted to make certain she understood him, "is if the *ton* discover that I am here with you and Lady Newfield, that I am residing here, then there will be questions as regards *our* acquaintance, Miss Sussex." His eyes were gentle. "And I do not want that."

Julianna's breath caught as she looked into his eyes, seeing something there that she had not seen before. He wanted to protect her, to keep her safe from his rather dire reputation.

"Miss Sussex," Lord Altringham said, his voice barely louder than a whisper and filled with something she could not quite understand. "I cannot have your reputation stained by my own. It would not be fair."

Without meaning to, Julianna reached out across the table and placed her hand over his. Lord Altringham started violently at her touch, surprising her by the force of his reaction, but she did not pull her hand away. Instead, she kept it there, feeling the urge to keep the connection and finding her heart quickening all the more as he looked into her eyes.

"Miss Sussex," Lord Altringham said, swallowing hard. "You must know that there is a connection between us. Surely you must feel it, in the same way that I have begun to." Lifting his other hand, he set it over hers. "I have found it very strange, if I am to be truthful, for I have never had these emotions for any other lady of my acquaintance before." He closed his eyes, his jaw working hard for a few moments. "And I do not know what to do with such feelings."

Julianna did not know what to say, tingles running up her arm from where his hand touched hers. Her breathing was quickening, her heart thumping so loudly she was certain he could hear it. When he lifted his head and looked into her eyes, she could barely breathe.

"But I have come to realize," he continued, his voice a little stronger now, "that I can do nothing, Miss Sussex."

Her own voice was hoarse. "What do you mean?"

"I—I mean that there is nothing between us that can be continued," he said tersely, as if he were battling within himself. "I am sorry, Miss Sussex, but there is something about me that I have not yet told you. Something, in fact, that I have tried my utmost to forget, to the point that I almost managed to entirely throw it from my mind."

She knew what he was going to say then, knew why he was pulling away from her—and her heart filled with joy. Had he been the very same gentleman she'd known from the first, then he would have thought nothing of trying to continue on with their acquaintance, even if he was already married to another. But now that he had begun to change, he clearly could not do as he wished any longer. Julianna felt a small smile pulling at her mouth, in direct contrast to the haunted expression that Lord Altringham bore.

"I am wed, Miss Sussex."

The words were wonderful to her ears, her fingers tightening on his.

"I know, this must be something of a shock to you, Miss Sussex," he continued, his eyes now on the table rather than on her face, "but I am wed. It took place only a short time ago and I confess that I have treated my wife with nothing more than disdain and cruelty." His eyes slowly lifted to hers and Julianna pushed the smile from her lips, wanting him to finish saying all that he wished before she herself said anything in return. Lord Altringham took in another long breath, his eyes squeezing shut for just a moment as though he were attempting to find the strength to keep speaking with such clarity.

"I do not think that she has anything to do with all that has occurred, however," he continued, his voice steadier now. "She is at my estate, waiting for my return." His lip curled. "I have been the worst sort of husband, thinking only of myself and forcing my wishes upon her." Looking back into her face, Julianna noted the color rising in his face and realized that he truly did feel a sense of shame. That also added to her relief and happiness, feeling as though her husband was, in fact, truly becoming a changed character.

"What is your wife's name?" she asked, as though she did not know anything about her and was seeking to discover more. "What does she look like? Is she a beauty?"

Lord Altringham did not immediately answer but instead, pulled his hands from hers and rubbed them both down over his face. Julianna slowly pulled her hand back, suddenly aware that she would have to tell him the truth about her own identity very soon and feeling a sheen of sweat break out on her brow.

"The truth is, Miss Sussex, I know nothing about her save her name." He shook his head. "She is not a beauty, from what I know, but if I am honest, I will tell you that I have no knowledge of what she looks like for I made quite certain to give her not even a modicum of my attention during our wedding." His hand curled into a fist and suddenly, out of nowhere, he thumped it down on the table, his brows furrowing and his mouth pulled tight. "I was cruel, Miss Sussex. I blamed her in some way, even though it was my own actions that brought us together. And then I returned to London in the hope that I would be able to continue on with my life just as it was before, whilst fully intending to forget her."

Julianna gave him a small smile. "I see. And you have decided that you should return to her?"

"Not as yet," Lord Altringham said firmly. "I cannot leave immediately without making certain that all of this has come to an end. I will not take danger back to my estate. She has already put up with a good deal from me and I will not add to her burden."

"And you will not continue with our acquaintance either," she added, surprised at the wretchedness that flung itself into his expression as he looked back at her. "That is the truth now, is it not?"

Lord Altringham hesitated, then nodded slowly. "That is the truth, Miss Sussex," he said, his voice low and quiet. "It is not the sort of thing that a gentleman such as I usually does, but you have brought out something within me that wants desperately to change." Shoving one hand through his hair again, he let out a ragged breath. "If I were not discovering a new part of me, Miss Sussex, I would not have given my wife a second thought. And yet, because of you, I find that I can do nothing other than that."

Julianna let out a long breath, feeling a swell of relief course through her. Closing her eyes, she felt the corner of her mouth lift in a small smile, despite the fear that came with the knowledge that she had to tell Lord Altringham the truth. There was so much in what he had said, such a wonderful, astonishing revelation, that she felt herself filled with delight, knowing now that the future for both herself and Lord Altringham would not be the dark, depressing one that she had first feared.

"You are smiling at me."

She opened her eyes and looked at her husband, seeing the confusion on his face and aware of what she had to do. "I am pleased with what you have said," she told him honestly. "To hear you speak with such consideration, to give your wife the respect she deserves rather than intending to push her from your thoughts—those things are all quite wonderful, Lord Altringham."

His confusion did not shift. "But that means that you and I cannot continue with what might have been a wonderful acquaintance," he said slowly, his brows furrowing together. "I thought that you..." His eyes widened, his brows lifting. "Wait, I have been hasty, have I not? You have never once said that there was something in your heart similar to what I have spoken of." His eyes slammed shut as he screwed up his face. "I have been foolish again, have I not?"

"No, no," Julianna exclaimed hastily, and Lord Altringham looked back at her, his expression now forlorn, his hazel eyes dull. "No, that is not what I mean, Lord Altringham. You misunderstand my smile."

A small flicker of hope pierced through his confusion. "What is it that you mean, Miss Sussex?"

Now was the moment for her to speak the truth, for her to tell him everything and to pray that he would understand. Her whole body began to tremble as she prepared herself to speak. The intensity in his eyes made her catch her breath, the air shuddering out of her as she tried to think of what she should say.

"Lord Altringham," she began quietly. "The reason I smile is because I am truly grateful to hear you speak of your wife—to speak of me—with such consideration."

She said nothing more, watching him as he frowned, clearly trying to understand what she had said. Her lips pressed tightly together, her fingers entwined in her lap.

"What is it you are trying to say, Miss Sussex?" he asked slowly, his brows knotting together. "You say I have spoken of *you* with consideration?"

Nodding, Julianna closed her eyes and forced the courage to rise up within her, letting out another shaking breath before she spoke. "I am not Miss Sussex," she said hoarsely. "There is nothing wrong with you remaining here, Lord Altringham. In fact, you have every right to join me in my bedchamber and reside there if you wish it." Opening her eyes, she saw his instant shock over what she had said, his eyes widening all the more as understanding hit him hard. "I was Miss Julianna Martins but I am now Lady Altringham." She took in another long breath. "In short, Lord Altringham, the lady you see before you now is none other than your wife."

CHAPTER TEN

Thomas could not breathe. His eyes were fixed to Miss Sussex, his stomach filled with knots of tension, his hands tightly folded into fists as the truth of what she had said finally washed over him.

Miss Sussex was not Miss Sussex after all, it seemed. The lady he had come to think of in a much warmer manner than any other, the lady who had been the source of his confusion and doubt these last few days, was none other than his wife.

His wife.

"I—I do not understand," he said, his voice barely loud enough for even himself to hear. "You are my wife?"

"Yes."

"Miss Sussex, I—"

"Lady Altringham," she said gently. "I stood beside you in church and made my vows, Lord Altringham. I did not ever expect you to send me back to your estate without attending there yourself. That came as something of a shock, I confess, but I had Lady Newfield with me, for which I shall forever be grateful."

Thomas could not quite understand all that she was saying, his head buzzing loudly as thought after thought crashed into each other. He had been speaking with, confiding in, and enjoying the company of a lady he had thought to be a stranger to him, but who now he had come to learn was, in fact, his bride. The lady he had stood next to in church, who had spoken in such a tremulous voice when she had made her vows and whom he had turned away from in order to return to London... it was she who now sat opposite him, her eyes fixed to his and her lips pressing into each other, her tension rippling through her and out toward him.

She was waiting for him to react, he realized, his breathing now beginning to quicken. She was waiting for him to say something, to tell her the truth of how he felt, but he could not find anything to say.

"Lady Tillsbury is greatly concerned." Lady Newfield swept back into the room, the door closed tightly behind her as she hurried toward the table. "She heard what had happened to you, Lord Altringham, and realized that Miss Sussex and I might have been involved, given that our absence came shortly after you had been attacked."

Unable to say anything in response, Thomas tried to lift his gaze from Miss Sussex—Lady Altringham, he reminded himself—but found that he was quite unable to do so. It was as though a cloud had filled the room, covering everything except himself and his wife.

My wife.

The words were like heavy weights coming to rest on his shoulders. Oh, just how cruelly he had treated her! How disrespectful he had been! Shame covered him as he remembered all that she had seen of his behavior, all that she had witnessed. Quite why she had chosen to remain by his side, standing there when he struggled with the attacks that had been carried out against him, coming to warn him about the theft of his diamonds—he could not understand why she had done such a thing. Ought she not to have been removing herself from him? To be berating him for what he had chosen to do, for the foolishness he exhibited? Instead, she had said very little but had borne the pain with as much grace as she could, trying to help him regardless of what she felt and regardless of the hurt his actions had caused her.

"Ah." Lady Newfield looked from Thomas to Lady Altringham and back again. "I see that you have told him the truth, then."

"I have." Lady Altringham's voice was thin, shaking slightly as he saw a fear in her eyes he could well understand. Still, he could not tell her that all was quite all right, that he understood it all, for the shock of it was running through him, sending his heart into a furiously pounding beat.

"You must understand, Lord Altringham," Lady Newfield said firmly, sitting down close to them both. "This was my suggestion. Not at the first, of course, for my first intention was to take Julianna back to London to remind you that you had a duty to your wife."

"Then why did you not do so?" he asked gruffly.

Lady Newfield looked astonished, glancing toward

Lady Altringham, who, to his surprise, now appeared to be a little angry rather than upset or afraid.

"If you will recall, Lord Altringham," she said, her voice no longer shaking. "On our first meeting after our wedding, you did not recognize me." Her eyes narrowed as she looked at him angrily. "Do you not recall? We met at a soiree and you did not even have a *flicker* of recognition in your eyes!" She slammed one hand down flat on the table, making him start with surprise. "I came back to this townhouse and cried over the sorrowful future I now had laid out before me. I had a husband who did not recognize me, who did not care one fig about me, who believed that I was back at his estate so that he could continue living just as he pleased here in London. I have spent years under my father's harsh rule, being told what I must do and where I must go, without having any consideration for my needs or my desires. And to find myself married to a gentleman who himself held so many of the same traits as my father made my heart break into a thousand pieces."

"And that is where I suggested that we ought to take a different path," Lady Newfield added, her quiet voice bringing a calm to the room. "I suggested that she become Miss Sussex with myself as her chaperone. Were anyone to ask, they would simply be told that she was under my care and that I myself was a good friend of her parents." Lady Newfield shrugged. "Lady Tillsbury and Miss Glover were the only two who knew the truth of her identity."

Thomas shook his head, confusion blurring his

thoughts. "But what of the soiree?" he said slowly. "You were present there. Did no one seek an introduction?"

Lady Altringham gave him such a searching look that Thomas felt himself flush with embarrassment, as though he had said something so foolish that he ought to be ashamed.

"Do you not understand, Lord Altringham?" Lady Altringham asked after a moment. "Do you know nothing about the lady you married?" She closed her eyes, taking a moment before she answered. "My father is a foolish, debt-encumbered gentleman. I have spent any time I have had in society hiding away, making certain that no one sees me for fear of the ridicule that will be sent my way. I am not known to society. I am not discussed or spoken of. Thus, I sought out no introductions that evening and, with the sole intent of having you and I converse for a time, Lady Newfield did not encourage introductions either." She waved a hand. "And once you met me and I realized that you did not know who I was, I wanted to leave at once. And so we did."

Shame continued to fill him as he closed his eyes, remembering how he had met the lady he had thought to be Miss Sussex, without even having a single instinct that he had met her before.

"I see," he said heavily. "And so the ruse continued."

Lady Newfield poured some tea into both her own cup and Lady Altringham's cup also. Stirring it with her teaspoon, she waited until Thomas had looked up before she spoke.

"Was it wrong of me to think that you would be eager to be closer to a young lady who had no connections, engagements, or the like?" she said, one eyebrow lifted as she gave him a somewhat haughty look. "My only concern has been Julianna. I wanted her to have a life that was not a repeat of the one she has endured under her father."

Thomas nodded slowly, closing his eyes for a moment before opening them again. It felt as though the floor had opened up beneath him and he had fallen into a deep pit that was slowly squeezing him until the life left his body. His throat was tight, his chest painful as he dragged in air, finally able to accept all that Lady Newfield and Lady Altringham had told him.

The guilt he felt was enormous. It overwhelmed him, his shoulders slumping as he tried to look at Lady Altringham, only to see that she was staring steadfastly down at her teacup, stirring it absently.

"What was your intention in all of this?" he asked, willing her to look up at him. "What was it you wanted to achieve?"

Lady Altringham looked at him, a heaviness in her expression that made him wince. He was the cause of all of this, he knew, and yet he still had a good many questions.

"I wanted you to know me," she said softly, her words burning him. "I wanted you to know the lady you married, to find an interest in me that you might not have had otherwise."

He could not help but think that there was sense to this decision, to this way of thinking. When he had first married, he had not had any interest in his wife, and on his return to London, he had done all he could to throw her from his mind. He had done this so successfully that he had all but forgotten about her until only a couple of days ago.

"I am not a beauty," Lady Altringham continued, her voice holding no sadness but rather a practicality that he found to be deeply sorrowful indeed. "I did not know how I would garner your attention, but my grandmother encouraged me to find courage deep within myself. It was this newfound courage and strength that helped me further our acquaintance that night of the ball."

"The night that Lady Darlington sought me out," he muttered, seeing the flicker of pain in her eyes.

"Indeed," she answered stiffly. "I hoped, I suppose, that should it come to it, you would discover that I was not as other young ladies are around you." One shoulder lifted. "But then there was the carriage and the diamonds and our acquaintance grew from that instead."

Rubbing at his forehead with the palm of his hand, Thomas let out his breath in a whoosh. "I would never have asked you to do something inappropriate, Lady Altringham," he said honestly. "I knew from the start of our acquaintance that there was a difference between you and the other ladies of the *ton*. On top of which, I also discovered that I knew more about you than any other lady, and that I *wished* to know more." He shook his head, his gaze darting to Lady Newfield, who was drinking her tea in a very calm manner, as though this were merely a very pleasant morning conversation. "You say you are no beauty, Miss Sus—Lady Altringham, but I find that you have more beauty than any other lady of my acquaintance."

Something like relief washed over him as she lifted her eyes to his, feeling himself both rebuked, ashamed, and glad in equal measure. His tumultuous thoughts began to calm themselves, his heart no longer thumping in a furious manner as he looked into Lady Altringham's face and found himself almost happy that he was wed to her.

"I need not have any further confusion about all that I feel," he continued as she held his gaze, her eyes a little damp. "You have confused me greatly, I confess, for I have felt strange emotions that have never before flooded my heart. But yet, with being wed, I told myself that, in changing the sort of gentleman I was, I had to be respectful of both you and her. But now..." he closed his eyes, his lips curling slightly, "now I find that the lady I have had strong feelings for and my wife that I know so little about are, in fact, one and the same. And my heart is filled with relief because of it."

Lady Altringham lowered her head and he saw a tear slip from her eye and drop on the table. His heart lurched and he felt the urge to go to her at once, to rush to her side, take her hand, and hold her tightly so that the pain would not linger within her heart.

"I am sorry for the pain I have caused you," he said hoarsely, a sense of shame flooding him all over again. "I cannot imagine what you must have felt when you saw me with Lady Darlington." He swallowed hard. "The only thing I can assure you of is that I have done nothing, much to Lady Darlington's displeasure."

Lady Altringham's head lifted and she held his gaze, her eyes a little red.

"I speak the truth," he told her honestly. "I have not stolen a kiss from any lady since my return to London—since the day of our wedding. I have been given many opportunities by Lady Darlington, but I have not—"

"And Lady Guthrie?"

Heat flooded his cheeks. "Again, another time that I must have pained you," he said quietly. "The diamonds were for her as a gift to bring our acquaintance to an end." He shrugged, lifting one shoulder. "No one else was aware of my intention save for myself, but that is the truth." Wincing, he let out a small sigh. "I have not done such a thing as yet since the diamonds have not been found or returned to me, but I swear to you, Lady Altringham, that I shall do so without hesitation now."

Lady Altringham pressed her lips together, her head tilted just a little as she studied him. He could not tell what she was thinking, and he prayed that she would believe him, that she would trust him, but from the heavy sigh that escaped from her, he doubted that his hopes would be rewarded.

"I confess that I have noticed a change in you that I have been thoroughly delighted to see," she said, her voice so quiet that he struggled to hear her. "I have been very afraid of speaking to you, of telling you the truth, for I did not know how you would react." She looked toward Lady Newfield, her lips finally pulling into a smile. "My dear grandmother's advice has been proven correct, it seems."

He looked at Lady Newfield with curiosity. "Advice?"

Lady Newfield shrugged, her lips twisting slightly. "I

told my granddaughter that a gentleman who was aware of his behavior and willing, perhaps, to change such things, would be more willing to listen to what she had to say than one who had no concern over how he lived."

Thomas nodded and smiled back at her ruefully. "That is wise advice indeed, Lady Newfield," he admitted. "I would not have listened to you should you have spoken to me even a few days ago, Lady Altringham. In fact, I am sure I would have reacted in a most unfavorable manner."

"Then I am glad I waited," came the reply. "I am sorry for keeping the truth from you, Lord Altringham, but it was necessary."

"*More* than necessary," he said firmly, seeing himself just as she must see him and finding the reflection to be both ugly and twisted. "You are an incredibly brave and courageous young woman, Lady Altringham, and I speak truthfully when I tell you that I am honored to be your husband." He held one hand out to her across the table. "I swear that I shall do all I can to improve myself all the more from this day forward."

Seeing the way her eyes widened and her mouth opened just a fraction, Thomas knew that he had surprised her with his words, but he did not regret saying them. There was no dishonesty in what he had said, for he meant each and every word without even a twinge of regret. It was as though he had been given another opportunity to live his life, to live as a gentleman ought. And he had only Lady Altringham to thank.

"I suppose the question now is what are we to do next?" Lady Newfield interrupted, smiling brightly at him, her eyes gleaming and her cheeks now holding a little color. Evidently, she was just as relieved as he.

"What do you mean?" Lady Altringham asked, her own features still rather pale. "What can you be thinking of?"

Lady Newfield lifted one hand. "Well, we are not about to find out who is responsible simply by sitting here and discussing matters now, are we?" she said with a small smile. "Whilst I am very glad indeed that you have been able to tell the truth and that it has been met so amiably, that does not help us discover the truth, does it?"

Thomas felt a strange sense of protectiveness rise up within him. "I do not want you to worry about such things on my account, Lady Altringham," he said, the name still unfamiliar to his tongue. "I am sure I will be able to remove to my estate without much difficulty, so that we might—"

"Remove to the estate?" Lady Altringham interrupted, sounding incredulous. "That cannot be the correct decision, Lord Altringham. For what if danger follows you there where we are entirely alone?" She shuddered violently, her eyes closing. "For I do not want to be the one discovering you in an even worse state than you were last evening. If I am alone, then I shall not be able to be of much assistance!"

"My granddaughter is correct," Lady Newfield said, her words firm and decisive so that he felt he had no other choice but to listen. "We must discover the truth. To leave things as they stand at present leaves no resolution. If the danger follows you to your estate, then what will you do? Return to London in order to escape it?" She shook her head. "No, indeed. The truth must come out now, so that the situation is brought to an end. Only then will I feel contented in allowing my granddaughter to return to the Altringham estate with you."

Still feeling a grave warning in the depths of his heart, Thomas hesitated, pressing his lips together as he tried to find a way to explain himself. "I am only concerned for the safety of your granddaughter, Lady Newfield," he said quietly. "For once the *ton* know who she is to me, then surely the danger could pass to her also?"

Lady Altringham lifted one hand. "Then I shall not be 'Lady Altringham' to them," she said simply. "It is not difficult for me to continue on as 'Miss Sussex' for a time."

Something within Thomas rebelled at this. It was as if he wanted to tell all the world that Lady Altringham was with him here in London, to show her to the *ton* and declare just how deeply he cared for her. To have her continuing on as Miss Sussex did not sit well with him, yet he knew that it would be the best way to keep her safe.

"I think you will find us quite determined," Lady Altringham continued, her voice gentle as he looked into her face and wondered why he had ever thought her plain. Her blue eyes were light in color and swirling with what appeared to be flecks of light. Her fair hair framed her face, the gentle curls at her temples softening the way it had been pulled back. He suddenly recalled how he had seen her with her hair flowing around her shoulders, the pins pulled from it, and his breath hitched as that vision of her floated in front of his eyes.

There was more depth, more beauty, and more loveliness to this lady than in any of his previous acquaintances.

"Lord Altringham?"

He cleared his throat, a little embarrassed to have been caught so lost in thought. "You are quite correct to state you are determined," he said, seeing how Lady Altringham smiled a little self-consciously, glancing away as she did so. "And I know that such determination has been hard-fought."

"It has indeed," Lady Newfield said with an approving look. "Well, Lord Altringham, if you are resolved to continue on with this as we are at present, do you have any thought as to what we might do next?" Her brow furrowed. "How are we to find who stole your diamonds and who, most importantly, is so eager to take your life from you?"

Letting out a long breath, Thomas's lips twisted as he tried to think of what he could suggest. "There are, I am afraid, a good many gentlemen who would wish to take my life from me, given the sort of gentleman I am," he said heavily. "I will not pretend otherwise."

"But would any of them be so desperate to punish you as to try and kill you?" Lady Newfield asked, still speaking in the same blunt manner as before. "One rake can differ from the next in terms of the sort of ladies they might seek out."

Seeing how Lady Altringham blushed, Thomas felt

his own heart twist as he recalled the many ladies he had sought attentions from. "The truth is, Lady Newfield, that I have stolen affections from many a lady," he said honestly, thinking it best to speak truthfully and without pretense, given that Lady Newfield and Lady Altringham knew his reputation already. "But I have always stayed away from those who are already wed." He shrugged, aware of the heat that was steadily climbing up his spine. "It may sound foolish, given that my reputation is so poor already, but I have always determined never to seek out a lady who has already attached herself to a gentleman."

"Even if she is only courting?" Lady Altringham asked, her eyes not quite meeting his. "What then?"

Wincing, he spread his hands. "I do attempt to stay away from such ladies if I know that an engagement is due to take place," he said, seeing the redness of her cheeks and knowing that the same color was in his own face. "I am not a man of great moral character, Lady Altringham—that is to say, I have not *been* a man of great moral character, although I do hope that will change now."

"That does not help us when it comes to considering which gentlemen might wish to take your life from you," Lady Newfield stated, sounding a little frustrated. "There have been none that you have wronged in partic- ular? None whose sisters might..." Leaving the question unfinished, she looked at Thomas with a slightly tilted head, but he only shook his head.

"Then the diamonds," Lady Altringham said with a sigh. "Is there something there that we might consider?

You have said, Lord Altringham, that you have not yet questioned your staff. Is that not so?"

"Yes, indeed!" he exclaimed, seeing the chance that now lay before him, the chance to do *something* that could help with such difficulties. "Lord Fairfax suggested that my driver might have been approached and given a small sum of money in order to ignore the fact that I was being robbed."

Lady Altringham nodded. "I can understand that consideration," she said with a smile. "You say you have not spoken to anyone about your diamonds and your intention to give them to Lady Guthrie—but I am certain you would have made mention of it to your staff in order to make preparations. And some of them would be with you when you purchased the diamonds."

He let out a long breath, realizing that what she said was quite true. "Yes, indeed."

She smiled. "Then why do we not speak to your driver and ask him for the truth?"

"Do you think he will give it so readily, if he knows he will be thrown from his position if he does so?" Lady Newfield asked, the question making the smile fade from Lady Altringham's lips. "A servant's employment is their most important possession. If they tell you the truth, they will lose their position. If they lie, then they will be quite contented."

Thomas frowned. "Then I shall ask them to tell me the truth without fear of losing their position," he said, hating the very idea of keeping on a disloyal servant but knowing that he had no other choice if he were to find the truth. "That is all I can do."

Lady Newfield hesitated, then looked at him. "Can you recall if you spoke of Lady Guthrie to anyone else, Lord Altringham?" she asked quietly. "Do you know if any other heard of your intention to give your diamonds to the lady?"

Again, Thomas frowned, running one hand over his eyes as he struggled to recall. "I do not think that I..." His words faded away as he shook his head. "I did not mention the lady to anyone, save to Lady Darlington," he said eventually. "And even then, I did not say a great deal."

Lady Altringham and Lady Newfield exchanged glances.

"Lady Darlington knew of your connection to Lady Guthrie?" Lady Altringham asked, looking a little surprised. "She, who appeared to be very attached to you herself?"

Thomas, who thought nothing of Lady Darlington's jealousy, merely shrugged. "It does not mean anything. Lady Darlington is inclined to be a little jealous, that is all."

"I know very little about such things," Lady Altringham continued, now looking a little embarrassed, "but I have been informed that a gentleman is inclined to give small gifts to a lady such as Lady Guthrie. Is that not so?"

Aware that his face was hot with mortification—for it was not common for a gentleman to be discussing his mistress in such a calm manner—Thomas nodded and cleared his throat.

"And you would have given no such gifts to Lady

Darlington," she continued as he watched her become a little more animated in her speech, her hands thrown up in exclamation. "You say that she might very well be jealous, Lord Altringham—jealous of the gifts and the attentions you gave to Lady Guthrie!"

"I am sure it would not have taken a great deal of effort to have your staff speak of the diamonds and your intentions for them," Lady Newfield said. "Without meaning to speak unkindly, Lord Altringham, you have already said that you do not believe your staff to be particularly loyal to you."

A chill ran down Thomas' back as he looked from one lady to the next, seeing the understanding in their eyes. "My staff are not particularly loyal, no," he said, all the more embarrassed. "I do not treat them with any particular kindness and it is as you say, Lady Newfield." Again, he passed a hand over his eyes. "I am sure it would not have been of any difficulty for Lady Darlington to persuade my staff to speak of the planned trip to Lady Guthrie's townhouse the following day." He shook his head to himself. "She might, very easily, have left the ball early and gone directly to my townhouse in order to speak to my staff. After all, she was very angry with me."

"Oh?" Lady Altringham looked surprised.

"I brushed her attentions aside," he said, without wanting to go into a deep explanation of what had occurred. "On that occasion and then again last evening." His smile was rueful. "Had it not been a gentleman standing over me, I would have felt certain that Lady Darlington was the only person responsible!"

Lady Newfield let out a small laugh, which in turn made Lady Altringham smile.

"It seems we are to talk to your driver, Lord Altringham, and then to Lady Darlington herself," Lady Altringham said, her eyes holding a brightness that made his heart lift in anticipation, hopeful that this might bring to an end the struggles and difficulties that surrounded him at present. She glanced at his temple, her face now etched with concern. "Do you feel able to attend with us or should you like to remain here and rest?"

The answer was instantaneous. "Wherever you go, Lady Altringham, there you will find me," he said decisively, rising to his feet. "I should not dream of letting you go without my company. After all," he continued, walking toward her and holding out his hand so that she might take it as she rose from the chair, "it is because of me that these troubles have surrounded us, is it not?"

The way her hand moved toward his, the delicate hesitation of her touch, and the warmth of her fingers sent a flurry of feeling all through Thomas. He was robbed of speech for a moment as she came to stand by him, closer than she had ever stood before. Thomas was captivated by the curve of her mouth, the smile in her eyes, the gentle scent of rose teasing his senses.

"It is indeed *entirely* because of you, Lord Altringham," she answered, her voice low and quiet, "but given that we are now bound together as man and wife, I believe my place is directly by your side, no matter what we are faced with."

Without hesitation, Thomas lifted her hand to his lips and kissed the back of her hand gently. "You are quite remarkable, Lady Altringham," he told her, seeing the blush in her cheeks. "The sooner we can bring this to a close, the sooner I can begin to make amends for all the trouble I have caused you."

Lady Newfield cleared her throat as she stood by the open door, causing Lady Altringham's blushes to mount all the more.

"Then might I suggest we depart, before we waste any more time?" Lady Newfield asked, a smile in her voice. "Come, Lord Altringham, you will have time to make your prayers and petitions to your lady wife soon enough."

"Indeed I will," Thomas agreed, allowing Lady Altringham to step forward and through the door first, before he followed immediately after.

CHAPTER ELEVEN

"What is your driver's name?"

Lord Altringham looked back at her, his frown burrowing through his forehead, lines forming like deep grooves. It took him a few moments to answer.

"Stubbs, I believe," he said, a little embarrassed. "I cannot be sure."

Julianna did not immediately reply, seeing the shame in his eyes and choosing not to increase it by remarking that she considered it very odd indeed for a gentleman not to know the name of his driver. Lord Altringham had already stated that he was not a gentleman inclined toward kindness to his staff, although Julianna had no doubt that such a thing would change in the future.

"Stubbs, my lord."

Julianna gave Lord Altringham a quick smile, seeing the relief on his face as the man in question stepped into the room. He was broad and rather short, his shoulders slumped and his head forward. Behind him came a tall, thin man, who appeared to be a little younger than the first. He, too, had slumped shoulders and a lowered head, as though they were both afraid of their master.

She glanced at Lord Altringham, seeing his hazel eyes narrow slightly as they turned from one gentleman to the next. She could not imagine what he must be thinking at this present moment. Was he a little afraid about what was going to be revealed, perhaps? Or unsure as to whether or not he would be given the truth from these two men?

"Stubbs," he said as the man stopped a few feet away from him. "And Collins, is it not?"

The thin man nodded.

"I have asked you here to speak to you about Lady Darlington."

Julianna watched both men closely, seeing how the larger man started slightly, although he did not lift his head or give any indication that he recognized the name that had been spoken to him.

"Do either of you recognize that name?" Lady Newfield asked, with both men swiveling their eyes toward her for a moment, then dropping their heads again.

"Of course not, my lady," the driver said gruffly.

"No?" Lord Altringham replied, his tone of voice making it quite clear that he did not believe the immediate denial. He glanced at Julianna and she nodded, recalling what he had asked her to do prior to the two men coming in.

"If I might get your attention for a moment," she said, trying to inject her voice with as much confidence as possible. "I shall inform you now that I am the soon-to-be mistress of the Altringham estate, and that as such, I have a good deal of sway when it comes to your positions in this house."

Both men looked at each other, their eyes darting toward her for just a moment before dropping to the floor again. She did not believe his denial either, for she had seen the driver flinch when Lady Darlington's name had been mentioned.

"I have Lord Altringham's promise that you will both retain your positions," she continued, "but only if you speak the truth." She saw both men drop their heads a little more, their hands held tightly in front of them. Lifting her chin, she poured strength into her voice. "I am acquainted with Lady Darlington. I think it best that, for your own sakes, you speak the truth to Lord Altringham and to myself."

The men said nothing. In fact, they did not move. Instead, they simply looked at the floor, their shoulders all the more hunched as they tried to avoid her gaze.

"Look at me."

Her voice rang around the room, echoing around every corner. She herself was astonished by just how determined her voice sounded, but all the more surprised when both men glanced up at her at once, both appearing a good deal more anxious than before.

"Tell me the truth," she said firmly. "The truth that I already know." She held their gaze, her hands planted firmly on her hips, a figure of strength. "Do you know Lady Darlington?"

The driver cleared his throat but said nothing, whilst the thinner gentleman began to twist his hands over each other, looking at the driver before dropping his eyes to the floor.

"Did you say we will keep our position?"

"Collins," Lord Altringham said loudly, garnering the man's attention. "You shall have your position within my household for as long as you wish it, just so long as you speak to me the truth of what you have done."

Collins looked at the driver, who gave him a tiny shake of his head. It did not go unnoticed by Lord Altringham or by Lady Newfield, who both rose to their feet. The driver stepped back.

"She gave us money," Collins stammered, his face draining of color as Lord Altringham frowned. "Said we were to ignore whatever else happened the following day."

A breath of relief rushed through Julianna as she saw the driver put his head in his hands, a groan escaping from his mouth.

"I see," Lord Altringham said softly. "Did she ask you for anything else?" He took a step forward and the driver shrank back. "Did she ask you about anything that I might have purchased?"

"No." The driver shook his head, his voice shaking. "She didn't."

"Then what *did* she ask you?" Julianna asked as Lord Altringham stood firmly in front of the driver. "What was it you told her?"

Stubbs cleared his throat again, his voice so low that it was difficult for Julianna to hear him clearly. "She came to speak to me one night, whilst we were waiting for your return," he said hoarsely. "I didn't want to tell her anything, but she threatened to have me thrown from my position." He swallowed, a few moments of silence passing between them all. "She said she already knew that you were to visit Lady Guthrie the following afternoon," he continued, rubbing one hand over his eyes. "I was aware that you had stated the carriage was to be prepared the following day in the afternoon."

"And I told you that we would be going to the park and then for an afternoon call," Lord Altringham said, sounding angry. "And this was all told to Lady Darlington?"

"Yes, my lord," Collins said, whilst the driver remained silent. "And even with the threats, she gave us coin in order to remain silent the following day. I—I didn't know why or what was going to happen or where."

Stubbs cleared his throat for what was the third time. "When a man came to the carriage, we simply did as we had been told," he said, sounding as though he were making some sort of serious confession under pain of death. "We did nothing."

"I do not think, then, that Lady Darlington knew for certain that I would have such an expensive gift within the carriage, ready for Lady Guthrie," Lord Altringham said quietly, looking to first Lady Newfield and then to Julianna. "I believe she simply sent someone who would look inside in the belief that there would be something there."

The driver cleared his throat, sending a wave of irritation through Julianna. She looked at him expectantly, waiting for him to speak.

"I think Lady Darlington came to the house, my

lord," he said, daring a look at Lord Altringham, who stared at him in astonishment. "I heard that the moment the carriage left, Lady Darlington appeared and spoke to the butler and one of the footmen." He dropped his head again. "The footman, George, said that when she went back into her carriage, there was a fellow with her." He snorted lightly. "Foolish boy, thinking himself jealous over a lady who gave him nothing more than a smile."

Julianna felt shock wash over her. Lady Darlington had been bold and brash, coming to Lord Altringham's house, no doubt to determine whether or not he *had* taken a gift with him in the carriage that day. Once she had used her flirtations to discover what she needed to know, she had merely climbed back into her carriage and made her way to Hyde Park. The man within the carriage with her had done precisely what she had wished for him to do, making certain that the diamonds were soon within her care.

"I did think her jealous, but I did not think her so conniving," Lord Altringham murmured, sinking back down into his chair and waving a hand at the driver. "You are both dismissed."

The two men hurried toward the door, relief evident in their faces as they spun around—only to be halted again by another word from Lord Altringham.

"Should either of you—in fact, should *any* of my staff —ever think of behaving in such a way again, then have no doubt." He rose, pointing one finger at the two men, who stood, wide-eyed and fearful, before him. "Have no doubt that you will be thrown from my employ with no references and the truth about your disloyalty made known to the *beau monde* in its entirety." His lips pulled thin, his brows low over his eyes and anger filling each and every word. "Do you understand me?"

Both men bowed, muttering their understanding under their breath, their voices barely audible and fear in their faces as they looked, terrified, at Lord Altringham.

"I think they will become some of the most loyal staff a gentleman has ever had," Lady Newfield said sweetly as the door closed behind them both. "You have put fear in their hearts and now they shall never dare even to speak ill of you."

Lord Altringham shook his head. "I hope, in time, they will come to respect me as a good master," he said heavily, "rather than obey out of fear."

Julianna sat down next to Lord Altringham, looking at his features and seeing the sorrow in his eyes and the traces of anger in the tightness of his jaw and the lines in his forehead.

"I am sorry that our suspicions have been proven true," she said carefully. "I am sure that you did not want your close acquaintance to be the one who—"

"She is not my close acquaintance, Julianna."

It was the first time he had used her name and the intimacy of it drew her closer to him. Her breath caught at the hard look in his eyes, seeming to smack hard against the tenderness with which he had spoken her name.

"She is not my close acquaintance," he said again, as though this made things all the clearer. "I used her for my own benefits, as she used me." His eyes became troubled, perhaps seeing himself as he truly was for the very first time. "In one way, it does not surprise me that she has done this. It is to be expected. We—she and I—are both very selfish creatures in our own ways."

Silence rang around the room for a few minutes. Julianna let out her breath slowly, not sure what to say, or if she should say anything at all for fear of breaking this reverent quietness.

"We should go and speak to her at once, Lord Altringham," Lady Newfield said eventually, her voice low. "Do you know where she might be?"

Lord Altringham let out a small, sad laugh. "I will send her a note and she will be present within half an hour," he said, shaking his head. "Thereafter we shall have the truth in its entirety from her, I can assure you."

Julianna swallowed a sudden lump that had come into her throat, seeing the sadness and regret in Lord Altringham's eyes and feeling a strange urge to comfort him. In one way, she was glad that he was seeing himself and his acquaintances as they truly were, noting that to speak so openly of oneself meant that an honest reflection was taking place within. But at the same time, she felt sure that this would bring with it a great deal of pain. A pain that would, in time, lead to healing—of that, she was quite certain—but there was something about him enduring such difficulty that brought a pain to her heart.

She was free now to allow her emotions and her feelings to rush through her with abandon. Now that the darkness of her future had turned to light, she was able to look at Lord Altringham with fresh eyes. There was a hope, now, that he would begin to care for her, that their life together would be one of contentment and happiness. It was more than she had ever allowed herself to dream of and yet it was now a real possibility. She could hardly believe it.

〜

LORD ALTRINGHAM HAD BEEN QUITE RIGHT, Julianna mused as the door opened and the butler announced Lady Darlington. She had arrived within half an hour. Glancing across to Lady Newfield, she saw the lady's eyes narrow as she took in the young lady from where they sat. They were in the corner of the room, with Lady Darlington swirling past them toward Lord Altringham without so much as a glance toward them. Her attention was clearly fixed on Lord Altringham to the point that she had not even become aware of their presence.

"Good afternoon, Lord Altringham," Lady Darlington breathed, dropping into a deep curtsy. "I was *very* glad to receive your note."

Lord Altringham, who had risen to his feet, did not so much as smile.

"There is a very important reason I requested your company this afternoon," Lord Altringham replied, his voice low and his expression grave. "It is not what you might believe, Lady Darlington."

"No?" she laughed, running one finger down Lord Altringham's arm. "I was *sure* that you—"

"You stole my diamonds."

Julianna tensed at the blunt words from Lord Altringham, seeing how Lady Darlington froze. She caught her breath as Lady Darlington took a small step back, fearing that she would run from the house without having spoken of the diamonds. Clearly, Lady Newfield considered this to be a real possibility also, for she rose from her chair quickly and made her way to the door.

Lady Darlington let out a small shriek of surprise, turning around just as Lady Newfield rose.

"As I said," Lord Altringham murmured as Lady Newfield pressed her back against the door, a tilted smile on her face. "The diamonds, Lady Darlington."

Her hands pressed against her heart, Lady Darlington let out another whimper and looked for somewhere to sit. Lord Altringham took a step closer to her, and Julianna rose to her feet also.

"We have heard it from Lord Altringham's driver and his tiger," Julianna said, surprised that she was a little nervous when it came to speaking with such force to Lady Darlington. "They told us everything."

Lady Darlington staggered back but no one reached for her. Julianna wondered if it was more of an act rather than a genuine weakness, believing that the lady in question was simply playing at being overcome in order to garner sympathy from Lord Altringham.

"Why did you steal the diamonds?" Lord Altringham asked quietly. "Was it because you wanted them for yourself?"

Lady Darlington let out a harsh sob, one hand over her mouth, but still, no one went to her aid. Julianna saw the hard look on Lord Altringham's face, the bored expression that was slowly being drawn on Lady Newfield's, and realized that they both knew all too well Lady Darlington's manipulation. All she was doing was trying to escape this situation in any way she could without giving anything away.

Julianna drew in a deep breath, planting her hands on her hips and trying to speak with a good deal more authority. "Why did you steal the diamonds, Lady Darlington? I can assure you that your tears will do nothing but force you to remain here a little longer."

Lady Darlington stopped crying almost at once. Her eyes turned toward Julianna, who was astonished to see the dark malevolence that ran through the other lady's features.

"Who are you?" Lady Darlington spat, her eyes sparking with anger. "Why do you think you have the authority to—"

"Answer the question, Lady Darlington." Julianna was as astonished as Lady Newfield and Lord Altringham that she interrupted and spoke with such firmness, but it seemed to silence Lady Darlington. "There is nothing else for you to do other than speak the truth."

Lady Darlington's lip curled but she turned back to face Lord Altringham. "All you have done is furnish Lady Guthrie with gifts," she said angrily. "And yet you have taken a good deal from me without even the smallest amount of return from you!" She sniffed and lifted her chin. "I know that you have stolen a good many affections from other ladies also, even though you assured me that I was the only one that you thought of."

Julianna took in a deep breath, seeing Lord Altringham frown.

"And so you stole the diamonds for yourself," Lady Newfield said. "Very well done, Lady Darlington."

"Well, how else was I to have something such as that?" Lady Darlington huffed, her arms folded across her chest. "It is not as though I have many other gentlemen willing to seek me out for my attentions." Narrowing her eyes, she shot an angry look toward Lord Altringham, whose brows lowered all the more.

"If I might ask, Lady Darlington," Lord Altringham said quietly, but with a dark expression on his face, "who spoke to you of these other ladies? Who helped stoke your anger by telling you of them all?"

Julianna caught her breath, seeing Lady Darlington's face pale and realizing precisely what Lord Altringham meant by his question. She moved forward, seeing Lady Darlington turn toward the door, perhaps looking for a way to escape.

"Who, Lady Darlington?" Lord Altringham asked, his jaw tight. "I must know."

Lady Darlington let out her breath shakily. "I have no reason to tell you."

"You may keep the diamonds in return," Lord Altringham said, astonishing them all. "And have no fear that I shall tell anyone of your discrepancies. If you do not tell me the truth, however, then I shall tell all of the *beau monde* what you have done and you will be forced to return the diamonds to me."

Evidently, the threat of being so treated by the *ton* and having the diamonds within her own possession for good were enough for Lady Darlington.

"Very well," she said, moving toward the door. "Lord

Fairfax, he spoke to me of the other ladies of your particular acquaintance," she said, her voice high-pitched, her expression tight. "I was greatly distressed to hear of it."

Lord Altringham let out a long, slow breath, dropping his head a little and rubbing his forehead with his hand. "And might it be that you heard of my intention to visit Lady Guthrie from Lord Fairfax?" he asked slowly.

Julianna held her breath as Lady Darlington lifted her chin and looked at each of them in turn, her eyes narrowed. "Yes," she said with a small, dark smile. "Although he did not tell me about the diamonds. I had to deduce that on my own."

And with that, she opened the door and stepped out, her head held high with no sign of the broken, sorrowful young lady that had been there only moments before. Julianna let out her breath, turning around to look at Lord Altringham, who was, much to her dismay, still standing with his head in his hand.

"My lord," she murmured, moving closer to him and extending one hand toward him. He looked up and, to her astonishment, reached out and took her hand. He then pulled her to him, his hand tight to hers so that she was looking up into his face. Her heart squeezed tight at the expression on his face. His eyes were closed tight, his jaw working furiously and lines grooved deep into his forehead.

"What is it, Lord Altringham?" she asked, tentatively pressing her free hand against his heart. "What has troubled you so?"

Slowly, he opened his eyes and looked at her, his gaze deeply troubled. "I recall what was said to me by the man that attacked me in the gardens," he said quietly. "And now I have come to a most troubling conclusion."

Hearing footsteps behind her, Julianna felt rather than saw Lady Newfield come to stand closer.

"What is it you recall?" Lady Newfield asked gently. "What was it that was said?"

Lord Altringham let out a very heavy sigh. "He stated that I was unworthy." His lips twisted ruefully. "And it is not that I do not believe the sentiment but rather that the only person who has said such a thing to me before has been, in fact, Lord Fairfax."

Julianna couldn't breathe for a moment, her chest tight as she began to realize what it was Lord Altringham meant. "You believe it was Lord Fairfax who attacked you on these two occasions?"

He nodded, swallowing hard. "And who made certain that Lady Darlington was fully aware of my intentions as regarded Lady Guthrie," he said softly. "I am in no doubt." Shaking his head, he pulled Julianna a little closer still. "The perpetrator in question is none other than my friend, Lord Fairfax."

CHAPTER TWELVE

Thomas looked all around the ballroom as he walked further in, trying to appear just as nonchalant as usual. This was no ordinary evening, however. This was the evening when he would reveal Lord Fairfax's true intentions for him to all the other guests. The disgrace that would follow would bring Lord Fairfax's attempts to a swift end and would, in all likelihood, throw him from the *ton*'s good graces for a long time.

And yet, there was something within Thomas that did not want to do so. His friend—for that was how he still thought of him—had been one of his acquaintances for many years and Thomas still did not understand what had occurred to make Lord Fairfax behave so. What had he done that had brought Lord Fairfax to this point? What had occurred for his friend now to wish him dead?

"Good evening, Lord Altringham."

Thomas started visibly, berating himself as he did so. Swiftly, he dropped into a bow, looking at the young lady in question and seeing how she blushed as he did so. Her friend beside her giggled but Thomas found no pleasure in the sound. Rather, he found himself somewhat irritated, not wanting to be interrupted from his task.

"Good evening, Miss Brampton," he said with a small smile that did not, he knew, spread to his eyes. "I do hope you are enjoying the ball thus far?" Wondering silently where the lady's chaperone was, Thomas let out a small sigh as the lady blushed even deeper, before simpering and murmuring that yes, she was having a wonderful time but her only complaint was that her dance card was not yet full.

Again, Thomas sighed inwardly but recalled that he was expected to act just as he would normally do. Thus, he inclined his head and begged to see her dance card, which Miss Brampton held out to him at once, clearly having expected him to do so. He then sought introductions to the lady's friend, who turned out to be a Miss Stanhope, and wrote his name on her dance card also.

This done, he smiled to them both, bowed, and took his leave, knowing full well that both of their dances would go unfulfilled. He had no intention of dancing this evening and by the time the dances came around, he would already be gone from this place, he was sure.

"Already seeking out new acquaintances, then?"

Lord Fairfax' voice was the usual mixture of disapproval and bemusement. Thomas felt a surge of anger climb up his spine but he did nothing other than shrug, looking at his friend with one lifted brow.

"What do you expect?" he said, as nonchalantly as he could. "I am eager to dance this evening."

"Dance?" Lord Fairfax repeated, looking at Thomas

askance. "I hardly think it is merely dancing that you seek this evening."

Thomas forced a laugh, even though inwardly, he winced at such words, knowing that they would have been quite true had he still been the very same gentleman of only a few weeks ago.

"I presume this means that you have no intention to return to your wife, then?"

A reply stuck in Thomas' throat. He looked at Lord Fairfax in surprise, a little taken aback by such a question. Why had he remarked on something such as that?"

Lord Fairfax sighed, rolling his eyes as he did so. "Yes, yes," he murmured, waving a hand. "I know you will berate me for mentioning your lady wife, but I must confess some curiosity." He shrugged. "It is as though you are not even wed—and indeed, I believe half the *ton* does not recall your marriage either."

It took Thomas a moment to respond, forcing a smile as he spoke. "That is just as I wish it," he answered, trying to chuckle. "I would rather not recall my marriage and thus, I would hope that the *beau monde* would forget it also." He laughed again, hating the words that came from him. "Besides which, if they forget my betrothal and my subsequent marriage, then I am sure I shall have a little more attention from some of the ladies of the *ton* than if they recalled it!"

Lord Fairfax grimaced, his eyes a little hooded as he regarded Thomas. He made no remark but rather turned his gaze away after a moment or two, as though attempting to make his distaste quite clear.

"I know, I know," Thomas continued, waving a hand

and feeling tense inside as he saw the opportunity to speak the very words Lord Fairfax himself had thrown at him on previous occasions. "You believe me quite unworthy of my bride, do you not?"

It took all of his strength to keep his smile fixed to his lips, to have his easy manner strung to every part of his body, but it appeared to persuade Lord Fairfax. The man looked at him sharply, his eyes a little narrowed, but after a moment, he let out his breath and shrugged, turning back toward the dancers and seeming to ignore Thomas completely.

"Yes, indeed so," he muttered, as though he could not bear to even look at Thomas. "You are quite unworthy."

Thomas laughed and shook his head, as though he thought Lord Fairfax quite ridiculous. Out of the corner of his eye, he saw none other than Miss Sussex—Lady Altringham, as he now knew her to be—beginning to approach. With a warm smile, he beckoned her toward him. Now was the time to begin their endeavor.

"Good evening, Lord Altringham."

"Good evening, Miss Sussex." He inclined his head, then greeted Lady Newfield, who stood, ever watchful, as though she knew precisely what a gentleman such as he might intend. He presumed that, out of all the parts they had to play, this particular one, where she had to appear quite angry and irritated with him, would be one of the easiest. "And good evening to you also, Lady Newfield."

"Good evening, Lord Altringham." Lady Newfield's voice was cool. "You are not dancing this evening, it seems?"

"Whatever gives you such an impression?" he asked

jovially. "Indeed, I have every intention of dancing this evening. I simply have not yet stirred from Lord Fairfax's side in order to seek out different partners." His smile was quick as he turned toward Miss Sussex. "I am sure you would be able to help me with my situation as it is at present, Miss Sussex?"

She giggled, just as he had hoped, and handed him her dance card. Their fingers touched and Thomas felt his stomach twist, butterflies filling it as he looked at the lady and saw her blush. There certainly was a good deal of feeling between them, he realized, although now was not the time to pursue such a thing.

"There," he said with a broad smile as he handed her back her dance card. "The waltz and then the supper dance, I think."

"The supper dance?" Miss Sussex replied with a surprised look. "Oh, Lord Altringham, that is very kind of you indeed."

Smiling warmly, he bid them both good evening and then turned his attention back toward Lord Fairfax.

"It will not be difficult to pull such a lady out of doors for a short time after the waltz," he murmured, seeing how Lord Fairfax frowned and praying desperately that their plan would work. "Just so long as Lady Newfield does not follow us." Arching one eyebrow, he jabbed Lord Fairfax in the arm. "You might make certain that she does not?"

Lord Fairfax frowned, his lips pulling tight. "I do not want to be a part of any of your schemes, Altringham."

Thomas pretended to consider this for a moment, then shrugged as though it did not matter. "Very well," he said with a heavy sigh. "Then I shall just have to hope that Lady Newfield does not notice when I steal her charge away for a short time." He laughed again, the sound tasting all the more false on his lips. "Or if she does, that she will not find us until I have been able to achieve all that I wish." Grinning, he slapped Lord Fairfax jovially on the arm and took his leave.

Now all he had to do was wait.

"Do you think he will warn Lady Newfield?"

As they twirled around the dance floor, Thomas looked down at his wife, holding her a little more closely than he ought and finding himself quite taken with the beauty of her gentle eyes. "I am sure that he will," he said softly, relishing the feeling of having her in his arms. "You saw his face when we were greeting each other, I am sure."

Lady Altringham nodded, her lip caught between her teeth for a moment as she bit it, considering. "Yes," she said slowly, looking up at him. "Yes, I did. He did not seem pleased with you at all."

Letting out a small laugh, Thomas smiled ruefully. "Yes, that is quite so," he answered wryly. "Lord Fairfax has never approved of me. And yet, I am certain that this will be an opportunity he will be quite unable to ignore, given that he will be able to pull me free from you, courtesy of Lady Newfield, and thereafter, he will have his chance to try and steal my life from me for what will be the third time."

Lady Altringham sucked in a breath, her eyes widening with fright. "I must hope he will not be successful."

"As must I," Thomas answered with a small smile. "Indeed, Lady Altringham, you are quite extraordinary." He hesitated for a moment, finding his breathing becoming a little ragged as he continued to twirl the lady across the floor. "Most young ladies of my acquaintance, who have been treated poorly by me, would be more than eager for my punishment. And yet you..." Giving her a warm smile, he resisted the urge to lean down and capture her lips with his, knowing that it was not at all appropriate for such a moment. However, the desire was settling deep within himself, eager to pull her closer, to wrap his arms about her, and to kiss her with all the strange emotions that surrounded him now whenever he was close to her.

"You need not thank me again, Lord Altringham," Lady Altringham replied with a look of curiosity in her eyes, as though she wanted to understand precisely what it was he was feeling at the present moment. "Indeed, I will not have it." Smiling, she stepped back from him as the music came to a close. "I am glad that, in a strange way, this situation has brought us closer together rather than pushed us further apart."

He bowed toward her, then offered her his arm, which she took at once, gazing up at him with what appeared to be an adoring expression. "As am I," he murmured, feeling the same thankfulness and relief that had filled him since she had revealed to him the truth about who she was. "And I fully intend to continue with my commitment to become just as good and decent a husband as ever there was." Reaching across, he patted her hand with his free one, before leading her toward the French doors that were open and waiting. "In the hope that, one day, Lady Altringham, I might be deserving of you."

The gardens were dark and dimly lit, which normally, Thomas would have found to be very delightful indeed. It would have been a perfect setting in which to steal away one lady after another, to try and ensure he garnered as much attention from each one as he could in only one evening. Tonight, however, he felt tense, his breathing quickening and his hand tightening as it rested on Lady Altringham's.

"It is a little cool this evening."

Lady Altringham's voice was quiet, but a slight warning tinged her words. With a quick shake of his head as though to clear his thoughts and force himself onto the task at hand, Thomas cleared his throat and spoke in what he hoped was his usual warm and encouraging voice.

"If you are cold, mayhap you would allow me to put my arm about your shoulders to warm you a little."

Lady Altringham laughed, the sound a little uncertain, betraying her own nervousness. "I do not think such a thing would be appropriate, my lord."

Grinning in the darkness, he rested one arm around her shoulders, his fingers resting on the very top of her left arm as he pulled her closer. "But it is near darkness, my dear lady," he told her, relieved that the gardens were very quiet indeed. "Surely there can be nothing to concern you here at present."

She laughed again, the sound still as tense as before. "You are incorrigible, Lord Altringham."

"Miss Sussex?"

Lady Newfield's voice leeched out of the darkness and, even though Thomas had been prepared for it, he found himself starting with surprise, stepping back from Lady Altringham and dropping his hand to his side.

"Just where have you been?" Lady Newfield screeched, hurrying toward them, a shadow in the darkness. "How *dare* you leave my side when you know very well the sort of gentleman Lord Altringham is?" She did not look at Thomas but rather reached out both hands and tugged her charge away. "You are behaving in a disgraceful manner, Miss Sussex! We are to return home *at once!*"

Protesting loudly, Miss Sussex was led away by an angry Lady Newfield, leaving Thomas to stand alone, sighing heavily as he raked one hand through his hair. Quite certain that Lord Fairfax was watching him from somewhere, he took a few minutes before turning to head back to the ballroom.

A small sound to his right had him turning swiftly. Praying that Lady Altringham and Lady Newfield were somewhere nearby, he spun around to look into the darker parts of the gardens, where he was sure Lord Fairfax was hiding.

"Hello?" he called, seeing and hearing nothing further. With a shrug, he turned back toward the path, only for something—or someone—to grab at his arm and haul him into the shadows. A shout of surprise left his mouth as he was slammed back against something hard. Instinctively, he ducked and dropped to his haunches, shifting to his left as something hit the tree where he had been shoved. Catching his breath, Thomas lifted himself up slowly, his hands outstretched and his eyes searching the shadows for Lord Fairfax.

"Who's there?" he cried, praying that Lady Newfield and Lady Altringham were somewhere behind him as he turned, the tree now just behind him. "Who is it?"

Out of nowhere, someone shoved him backwards, hard, and Thomas fell back, losing his balance and hitting his head against the tree. Stars began to swim in his vision as he groaned, blinking rapidly as he tried to push himself up, but finding that he lacked the strength to do so.

"I told you, you were unworthy."

Lord Fairfax's hissed voice came from the shadows, making Thomas catch his breath. Even though he knew that it *was* Lord Fairfax, there was still something quite horrifying about hearing his friend speak with such disdain and fury.

"I *am* unworthy," he said, dropping his hands into the earth and trying his utmost to push himself up again. "I have no claim to be otherwise."

A hard laugh came from the darkness. "You will not live this time, Lord Altringham."

"I think that is quite enough, Lord Fairfax."

Relief flooded Thomas as the two ladies suddenly appeared beside him. He had not heard them come back along the path, nor had he heard them come into the darker part of the gardens. And yet suddenly, there they were, with Lady Altringham bending down so that she might remain by his side, before pulling him up with her, his legs buckling as he attempted to stand. His head had been dealt quite a few blows these last few days and he felt barely able to deal with the shifting pain that ran from one side of his head to the other.

"Lord Fairfax?" Lady Newfield said firmly. "You may as well step forward and make yourself known." She came to stand beside Thomas, one hand on his shoulder for just a moment as he felt his strength returning. "We are aware that it is you who has been attempting to kill Lord Altringham."

"It is quite true, Fairfax," Thomas answered, putting one hand to the back of his head and feeling it come away sticky with blood. Wincing, he pulled out a handkerchief and wiped his hand before pressing it to the back of his head. "We know that you are the one who has arranged these attacks upon me."

He held his breath, unable to speak anymore as he waited for Lord Fairfax to say something. Would the fellow run back to the ballroom, leaving their questions unanswered and leaving them to stand there alone? Lady Altringham stood closer to him, pressing her fingers through the crook of his arm so that she could hold onto him.

"What is it that you want, Altringham?"

Lord Fairfax's voice echoed from the darkness and Thomas took a small step forward, knowing that it would be best to answer truthfully.

"I want to know what you are doing," he said, wondering where Lord Fairfax might be. "And why."

Lord Fairfax's laugh was malevolent, sending a shiver up Thomas' spine.

"You know quite well that I think very little of your behavior," he said, coming out of the darkness and standing before the three of them, a wraith-like figure. "Why should it surprise you that I now seek nothing other than to knock some sense into you?"

"Except, that is not what your intention was," Lady Altringham said, her voice loud and without tremor. "You have tried to kill Lord Altringham on three different occasions, have you not? You have tried to shoot him, to kill him with a blow to the head, and this time...?" She shrugged, looking up at Thomas, the whites of her eyes visible in the gloom. "What was it you intended?"

Lord Fairfax laughed again and Thomas felt Lady Altringham shudder.

"There is a very sharp knife in my hand, Altringham," Lord Fairfax said without hesitation. "I should like not to injure Lady Newfield and Miss Sussex, so I ask them both to step aside."

Lady Newfield said nothing, but instead came to stand in front of Thomas, her arms folded. "I shall do nothing of the sort," she said firmly. "And you are a fool to ask such a thing."

Thomas wanted to reach out and remove Lady Newfield from his path, but even a light touch to her shoulder told him that Lady Newfield would not allow herself to be moved.

"Why do you defend such a gentleman?" Lord Fairfax laughed mirthlessly. "Surely you know the sort of fellow he is? After all, you have only just come to pull your charge away from him!"

"Just as you informed me, Lord Fairfax," Lady Newfield replied with a hint of irony in her voice. "But there is more to this situation than you might first think, sir. Perhaps we, too, are able to play a part in order to achieve our aims."

There came a long silence after this remark. Thomas felt himself about to speak a good many times, only to prevent himself by doing so out of sheer force of will. Straining to hear, he kept his eyes fixed on the shadow of Lord Fairfax, fearful that he might suddenly hear Lady Newfield let out a cry of pain as Lord Fairfax attacked her in order to reach him.

"Why do you have such an eagerness to defend Lord Altringham?" Lord Fairfax asked eventually, his voice filled with disgust. "You know he is nothing more than a rake and yet you—"

"Why do you seek to kill me, Lord Fairfax?" Thomas interrupted, not wanting Lady Newfield to reveal the truth to him yet. "What is it I have done that has brought you such anger that you no longer wish for life to thrum through my veins?" He pressed Lady Newfield's shoulder in an attempt to remove her from where she stood but she did not even flinch. Rather, she remained steadfastly in front of him, with Lady Altringham pressed to his side. Shame filled him. He did not deserve their protection and yet they gave it to him willingly. "I know very well that I have done plenty of things that are shameful, but to have my life taken from me seems a severe punishment."

Lord Fairfax let out a harsh laugh. "It is nothing less than you deserve," he said fiercely. "You have taken everything I ever wanted and been able to achieve success no matter what you have done. You do everything wrong, treat those about you unfavorably, take what you wish from the ladies who desire you, and yet you find the delight and the felicitations of the *ton* still turned toward you." He laughed again but the sound was darker now, holding anger and pain rather than anything of mirth. "You do all manner of evil and yet the *beau monde* welcome you to them as though you are a long-lost child."

Lady Altringham caught her breath, her hands tightening on Thomas' arm. "Then you are jealous of Lord Altringham?"

"Jealous?" Lord Fairfax sounded scornful. "That is not a word I should use. I am angry, yes. Angry that he has been able to achieve such success when he does nothing well, whereas I, who do everything that a gentleman ought, am given nothing but disdain by the *ton*." He laughed harshly again, his voice becoming tighter, his words flung toward Thomas like sharp, flaming arrows. "I even thought I should do something quite marvelous and seek a lady to wed who would have no hope of such a thing without my offer. That, I was sure, would bring me happiness and contentment. However, I soon discovered that I was not considered worthy enough and was turned away!"

Thomas frowned, hearing the anger and hurt in Lord Fairfax's voice and wondering at it. "You sought to become wed?"

"I sought to marry Miss Martins," Lord Fairfax

retorted sharply. "Not that you would recall such a thing."

Beside him, Lady Altringham let out a quick gasp, making Thomas realize precisely what Lord Fairfax meant. His chest grew tight as he stared into the darkness, wishing he could see Lord Fairfax better. "You mean to say that you sought to court Miss Martins, daughter of Viscount Fotheringhay?"

There came a moment of silence, before Lord Fairfax spoke again. "I did not know the lady, of course, but I heard that she was very much looked down upon, ill considered by the *ton*," he said airily, as though such a thing granted him some sort of superiority, despite his current attempt to kill Thomas. "I glanced at her once or twice and thought her satisfactory, so sought out her father."

"But he refused you," Lady Altringham breathed, her voice very hard to make out. "He refused you because you were not wealthy enough."

There came another momentary hesitation, and Thomas himself was quite certain that Lord Fairfax was astonished at the truth that came from Lady Altringham's lips.

"Indeed," came the slow reply, the word drawn out carefully. "It was quite ridiculous, of course, for who else would marry the girl?" He snorted. "And then, of course, I heard that she was to wed none other than you, Lord Altringham."

Thomas shook his head. "But that did not come from any sort of goodness," he stated, seeing now that there was more than mere jealousy in Lord Fairfax's heart. "I had no other choice but to do so."

"Yes, but it was the lady I had chosen!" Lord Fairfax explained furiously. "I may not have cared for her, may not even have *known* her, but I had determined to make her my bride so that she could have all the happiness a life as a wife and mistress could have. I thought that such a good act would set aside my... difficulties with how well you were treated by the *ton*. I thought that they might look more favorably upon me also, only for you to step in and do precisely what I could not." His voice had become edged with anger now, his words rapid, and Thomas felt his heart thump furiously, half thinking to forcibly remove Lady Newfield from where she stood in order to protect her.

"And so you decided to punish Lord Altringham for all the injustices he had done to others as well as, inadvertently, to you," Lady Altringham said with such a softness to her voice that it seemed to bring calm to the entire situation, allowing Thomas to breathe a little easier. "Is that what you are stating, Lord Fairfax?"

"Yes!" he shouted, and Thomas realized that the shadowy figure of Lord Fairfax was now beginning to move closer. "He did not deserve to live in contentment and happiness, whilst treating others with such disdain! He even left his own wife to languish back at the estate! I am sure that she would have thanked me should she have ever discovered my intention." He drew in a ragged breath. "An intention that has not left me yet."

Everything seemed to happen at once. Realizing that Lord Fairfax intended to lunge at him, Thomas shoved

Lady Newfield hard to one side, intending to protect her, only for Lady Altringham to scream and grab at his arm, pulling him in the opposite direction. Losing his balance, Thomas fell hard to the ground, his injured head knocking back against the ground. Groaning, he rolled over and tried to right himself, hearing Lord Fairfax screaming furiously as he tried to discover where Thomas was.

"You shall not have him!" Lady Altringham exclaimed, her voice loud over the top of Lord Fairfax's mutinous words. "I shall not allow you!"

Thomas pushed himself up slowly, his head thumping so furiously that for a moment, he thought he might pass out. Something knocked into him and he lurched back, his hands grasping at someone—only for something painful and sharp to pierce his shoulder.

Letting out a bellow of pain, Thomas threw his arms out and shoved hard at Lord Fairfax, just before the world around him began to spin. Dazed, he staggered back, forcing himself to remain upright.

"Julianna!" he shouted as more voices began to fill the gardens. "Julianna! Where are you?"

Falling back, Thomas could find no strength left within him. Resting his aching head on the grass, his eyes closed of their own accord, unconsciousness forcing him to return to that too familiar darkness once more.

His last thought, the last lurch of fear that ran through his heart, was for Julianna. Where was she? What had happened to her? Would he ever see her dear face again?

CHAPTER THIRTEEN

To see Lord Fairfax being dragged through the ballroom by two of his peers, with two others helping a half-conscious and clearly injured Lord Altringham through the room, had told Julianna that the *ton* were both horrified and astonished at what they had seen. There would be no place for Lord Fairfax in the *beau monde* now. Not after what some of the *ton* had witnessed.

"He will be quite all right," Lady Newfield said with a small smile on her face that did not quite have the reassurance that Julianna needed. "Although I confess that I am sorry he has been injured for what is now the fourth time."

Julianna nodded, hurriedly following the gentlemen as they helped Lord Altringham into a smaller room. Lord Fairfax was taken into another, but she could still hear him shouting and exclaiming that he had done precisely as Lord Altringham had deserved.

Shuddering at the vehemence in his voice, she clutched Lady Newfield's arm tightly.

"Was it correct what Lord Fairfax said?" Lady Newfield asked as she and Julianna came to a stop just inside the room and a footman hurried past them, a bowl of water and a cloth in his hand. "Did he ask your father to court you?"

Not certain she could trust her voice, Julianna nodded.

"I see," Lady Newfield said slowly. "But he did not recognize you, then?"

"I think it must be as Lord Fairfax said," Julianna answered, recalling how her father had told her that a gentleman had sought to court her, with the intention of taking her as a wife, but how he had thrown such a request aside, believing the gentleman to be less than suitable for her. By that, Julianna had known that her father had meant that the gentleman did not have enough wealth to satisfy him and, in her frustration and her grief, she had never once asked her father for the gentleman's name. Lord Fairfax must have been the gentleman, even if he had never once cared to seek her out. "He sought only to marry me in order to justify himself, to make himself appear great to the *ton*." She shrugged, trying to pretend that it did not matter even though the words Lord Fairfax had said had stung her. "That was all that he wanted. He wanted the same treatment as Lord Altringham has from the *beau monde*, thinking himself more deserving of it because of how well he appeared." Her lips twisted, her heart pained as she looked across at her husband, wanting desperately to go to him but knowing that she could do nothing. "I am sure that you are aware, as I am, that the *ton* practically fawned over my husband. Even though he was a rake and a cad, they welcomed him to their gatherings and tried to catch his attention with warm smiles and open arms." Sighing, she let go of Lady Newfield's arm. "I believe that Lord Fairfax felt the sting of unfairness, given that he is a—*was* an upstanding gentleman who did very little wrong. To be foiled in his intention to marry me by my father, only for Lord Altringham, the source of his frustrations, to then do so, must have angered him terribly."

"But that does not justify his actions," Lady Newfield answered, and Julianna shook her head fervently.

"Indeed, it does not," she answered, seeing how the footman was now dabbing at the wound, her face paling at the sight of her husband's bloodied shirt. "But that, I think, was his reason for doing as he did."

Lady Newfield tilted her head, thinking for a moment. "And telling Lady Darlington of Lord Altringham's other... interests was simply to make his life all the more difficult," she finished, and Julianna nodded. "Ah well, it is at an end now. Lord Fairfax will not be able to return to society as he had once done now that they have all seen his disgrace."

"And Lord Altringham?" Julianna whispered, a trifle hoarsely. "Do you think that he will recover?"

Her grandmother pressed Julianna's hand, holding her gaze firmly. "Your husband is a strong man," she told her decisively. "Have no doubt. Come the morrow, he will be up and about as usual."

It was not the following day, nor even the day after that, but three days after the attack that Lord Altringham finally managed to recover enough to rise and walk about in his usual manner. His head, having already received one blow, had been damaged again by this second blow. The injury to his shoulder—the one unharmed from the previous attack—had been superficial but took some time to heal, given that every time Lord Altringham moved his arm, the wound opened itself up again. This led to much frustration but in the end, he remained abed for two days, until, finally, he was able to rise.

Julianna had never been so glad to see him as when he was welcomed into Lady Newfield's house, clearly eager to be in her company once more. She could not help but rise and hurry closer toward him as he came into the drawing room, her eyes filled with worry as she looked up at him.

"Are you well, Lord Altringham?" she asked, careful not to set her hand on his shoulder but instead lifting it to his face, glad that Lady Newfield was not present at the moment. Running her fingers lightly over his cheek, she was astonished to see his eyes begin to glow, his cheeks flushing just a little as he pressed his hand against her own.

"I am well," he told her with such a tenderness in his voice that she wanted to throw her arms about his neck and pull him closer still. "I am not entirely healed but I am recovering, for which I am very glad."

"As am I," she breathed, holding onto his arm and

leading him into the room, gesturing for him to sit down. "Should you like something to drink.?" She stood hesitantly in front of him, wondering what he would ask for. "I can send for the tea tray."

He smiled at her, sitting down a little awkwardly on the sofa, one arm stretched out along it as though she ought to be sitting next to him. "Tea would be quite lovely, I thank you."

The kindness in his voice and the warmth in his eyes made her heart melt. Ringing the bell, she hesitated before going to sit down beside him, finding the distance between them now very little indeed.

"It is all at an end, then," he said softly, looking at her with such a depth in his gaze as though he could see directly into her heart and knew all that she was feeling. "Lord Fairfax is gone from London."

Julianna nodded, feeling a great deal of relief. "I received a note from Miss Glover this morning," she said, thinking how much she still had to tell her about. "She informed me that Lord Fairfax had quit the town, for all invitations to social gatherings had been rescinded and if he even stepped out of doors, he was given the cut direct from everybody." Her smile was a little lackluster. "I am sure it is for the best."

"Indeed it is," he answered, reaching across and picking up her hand. "You have a good heart, Julianna. You still feel for him in a way, I believe."

Twisting her lips, Julianna considered this. "I do not believe that he has done anything right," she said firmly. "Nor do I believe that the fault is entirely his." She held her breath, fearing that she might have insulted him, only for Lord Altringham to nod slowly.

"It is as he said," Lord Altringham admitted. "The *beau monde* thought far too well of me. They ignored my less than appropriate ways whilst continuing to seek me out." He shrugged. "I, of course, did nothing to temper that. Not until I met you." His voice had become softer now and as she turned to face him a little more, Lord Altringham reached up and brushed his fingers down her cheeks. Her skin began to prickle, her heart going a good deal faster than ever before.

"You have become more to me than any other," he told her gently. "Without you, I would have remained quite lost in my ways of arrogance and selfishness." He sighed and dropped his hand. "In fact, I might, even now, be no longer in the land of the living. My name might be carved on a stone, my body belonging to the earth."

Julianna shuddered and closed her eyes. "I am sure you would have—"

"No, Julianna," he insisted, interrupting her. "You have been more courageous than any I have known. Your strength has shown me my wrongs and I have found myself desiring to step away from all that I have once known." Shaking his head, he reached down and pressed her fingers, his hand tight to hers. "Were it not for you, I might never have changed."

She looked into his eyes, realizing that he had moved a fraction closer to her. Her breath hitched and she felt her stomach turn over, her anticipation mounting furiously.

"I intend to declare to all that you are my bride," he

said, leaning closer to her still, his mouth only a few inches from hers. "Already I have sent out the invitations. A ball will be held in three days' time, solely in your honor." Smiling at the surprise in her eyes, Lord Altringham let go of her hands but only so that he might cup her face gently. "You have saved me, and I want all of England to know of it."

She was ready for his kiss, lifting her head and closing her eyes in anticipation. Chest tight, barely able to breathe, she waited for his lips to touch hers—only for the door to open and Lord Altringham to let go of her in an instant.

Julianna flushed red as a maid came in with a tea tray, soon followed by Lady Newfield. She gave Julianna a knowing look, as only a grandmother can give to a granddaughter, and Julianna felt her cheeks burn all the hotter.

"Thank you for your kind invitation, Lord Altringham," Lady Newfield said, sitting down gracefully and gesturing for Julianna to pour the tea. "A ball sounds quite wonderful. And it is to be in your wife's honor!" Her eyes were all kindness, her delight at his obvious attentions to Julianna now lifting him in her considerations. "That is very good indeed."

"I was just informing Lady Altringham of what I have planned," Lord Altringham replied, somewhat hastily. "I am determined that the *ton* shall know her as I do, so that they can see just how blessed a gentleman I am. A gentleman who did not deserve such loveliness, such sweetness and affection, and yet has been granted it regardless." He smiled at her as their fingers touched, making Julianna almost drop the teacup. "The ball cannot come soon enough."

THE NEXT THREE days were spent in eager anticipation. Julianna spent almost every day with Lord Altringham, conversing and laughing together as husband and wife would do. He told her everything about his estate, everything about his life back in the country, and she listened with delight, beginning to look forward to returning to his estate with him. It would be a happy home now rather than a place of sorrow and fear. She had not come to live with him in his townhouse as yet, and he had not come to reside at Lady Newfield's either. He told her that this was simply so that no one in the *ton* would think poorly of her before the ball, which Julianna was greatly pleased with. The ball sounded quite wonderful, for it would be the first time that such a thing was simply in her honor, the first time that she would be able to hold her head high with nothing more than sheer delight and pride. But what was of the greatest significance was the way that she felt for Lord Altringham—for the way that her heart softened whenever he came into the room, for the joy that their conversation brought her. For the beginnings of love that were swelling up within her heart.

"MIGHT I say just how wonderful you look this evening?"

Julianna blushed as she looked up into her husband's face, aware that he truly did feel the admiration that was etched there.

"You are very kind," she told him as he bowed and offered her his arm in a most gentlemanly fashion. "You look very handsome." Her face colored at the way his eyes shot to hers and the broad smile that pulled at his lips at her compliment, but she meant every word with genuine honesty.

"This evening is all to be for your benefit," he told her fervently. "The moment we step into the ballroom, I shall have the orchestra cease their playing and shall make the announcement."

Despite her happiness at being on Lord Altringham's arm, Julianna felt her heart twist within her, her stomach swirling with nerves as she contemplated walking out in front of the *ton* and having them all looking at her curiously.

"There is nothing to worry about," Lord Altringham told her gently. "Truly, Lady Altringham—Julianna. Yes, there shall be a few stares and yes, the room will be rife with whispers, but all you must do is simply look into my eyes and fix your gaze there." Reaching up, he brushed her cheek with the back of his hand. "Might you be able to do that?"

She smiled at him, her stomach settling with the confidence in his eyes. "Willingly," she answered, and he laughed and pressed her hand to his lips, before tucking it under his arm and turning toward the door of the ballroom.

Julianna forced herself to lift her chin rather than

duck her head as she stepped into the ballroom with Lord Altringham. All about her, the noise of the guests seemed to quieten, only to rise again to an almost triumphant crescendo, as though they had been expecting to see Lord Altringham do something akin to this from the very beginning.

Lord Altringham smiled and nodded, and Julianna could see a few young ladies bat their eyelashes at him, smiling coquettishly, but Lord Altringham did not even give them a momentary glance. Juliette saw this and smiled to herself, feeling more and more confident with every step. She knew for certain that this man had begun to change before her very eyes. There was nothing she needed to fear now. Her future was bright. Their shared affection and determination to be all that the other needed would bring them both happiness and joy. She was proud to be standing beside Lord Altringham, proud to show all of England that the rake they once knew was now no longer.

The orchestra, seeing Lord Altringham approaching, soon brought their dance to a close. The dancers returned to their companions or their chaperones, and Lord Altringham led her forward to stand directly in the middle of the room, so that everyone could see them. As though the crowd knew that they were to remain silent, a quiet began to fall over the room, with every eye slowly turning toward them.

Julianna's heart began to quicken as she looked all about her, still holding tight to Lord Altringham's arm. In the crowd, she spotted Lady Tillsbury and Miss Glover. Both were smiling warmly at her and she returned their smile, albeit a little more tremulous than the ones they wore.

"Ladies and gentlemen, I must thank you all for attending this evening," Lord Altringham began, letting go of Julianna's arm and instead, capturing her hand. "This evening's ball is in celebration of a lady whom I have come to know very well indeed these last few weeks." He turned toward her, his voice still raised but his words directed solely at her.

"You have shown me my faults. You have shown me my flaws. And you have shown me the sort of character I now wish to be. I shall never again bear the name of 'rake'. I turn from that path entirely. Instead, I seek only to be yours. To live as a gentleman who is worthy of your affection, your devotion, and your strength. To be as I have never been before." Reaching out, he touched her cheek and then looked back at the crowd. "Ladies and gentlemen, might I present to you... my wife, Lady Altringham."

There was a moment of silence, and then the crowd erupted. Exclamations, cheers, applause, and shrieks of what Julianna supposed might be either delight or fury spread out across the room—but she did not turn to look at anyone. Instead, she kept her gaze fixed on Lord Altringham's face, looking up into his eyes and seeing something there that had never been present before.

"I think I am in love with you, my dear Julianna," Lord Altringham said softly, his finger tracing the curve of her cheek, running down her neck before brushing down her arm to capture her hand. "And I intend to ensure that every day of my life is spent proving that love to you."

Her heart was full, her eyes glistening with joyful tears. "As I shall do for you,...Thomas," she whispered, seeing the spark of happiness in his eyes as he realized what she meant. "For my heart is filled with love for you also."

Lord Altringham stared at her for a moment, then right in front of the crowd and without any hesitation, he pulled her tightly to him and pressed his lips to hers. Julianna did not hear the gasps of shock that came from around them. Rather, she melted into Lord Altringham's embrace, finding more happiness in that one moment than she had ever felt before.

I HOPE you enjoyed In Search of Love! Did you miss the first book in the Convenient Arrangements series, A Broken Betrothal? If you did, check it out on the Kindle store A Broken Betrothal

IF YOU HAVE READ this one, please read ahead for a sneak peek at The Duke's Saving Grace, one of my favorites from The Returned Lords of Grosvenor Square: A Regency Romance Boxset

Thank you for reading and supporting my books! I hope this story brought you some escape from the real world into the always captivating Regency world. A good story, especially one with a happy ending, just brightens your day and makes you feel good! If you enjoyed the book, would you leave a review on Amazon? Reviews are always appreciated.

Below is a complete list of all my books! Why not click and see if one of them can keep you entertained for a few hours?

The Duke's Daughters Series
The Duke's Daughters: A Sweet Regency Romance
Boxset
A Rogue for a Lady
My Restless Earl
Rescued by an Earl
In the Arms of an Earl
The Reluctant Marquess (Prequel)

A Smithfield Market Regency Romance
The Smithfield Market Romances: A Sweet Regency
Romance Boxset
The Rogue's Flower
Saved by the Scoundrel
Mending the Duke
The Baron's Malady

The Returned Lords of Grosvenor Square
The Returned Lords of Grosvenor Square: A Regency
Romance Boxset
The Waiting Bride
The Long Return
The Duke's Saving Grace
A New Home for the Duke

The Spinsters Guild
A New Beginning
The Disgraced Bride
A Gentleman's Revenge
A Foolish Wager
A Lord Undone

Convenient Arrangements
A Broken Betrothal
In Search of Love

Christmas Stories
Love and Christmas Wishes: Three Regency Romance
Novellas
A Family for Christmas

Mistletoe Magic: A Regency Romance
Home for Christmas Series Page

Happy Reading!

All my love,

Rose

A SNEAK PEEK OF THE
DUKE'S SAVING GRACE

CHAPTER ONE

"Ah, here comes my bride to be!"

Miss Deborah Harland laughed softly as she walked towards one of the many injured soldiers that now occupied the abbey's chapel. "Now then, Mr. Griggs, you know very well that I could not possibly accept your kind offer," she said, teasingly. "For whatever would Mr. Hunter do then?"

She gestured towards Hunter, who lay on his side in the bed opposite, although, to Deborah's relief, he smiled at her as she looked at him. He seemed a little better today.

"That's true," Mr. Griggs replied, his eyes twinkling as he sat back against the pillows. "But still, you know that I'd give up my friendship with Hunter to make you my wife."

"And I am truly touched," Deborah replied. "But I think that you and I must remain friends for the moment, Mr. Griggs. You and Mr. Hunter have got a life to return to, once you're fully recovered, and I have a life here that I need to consider."

Mr. Griggs winced as she slowly began to unwrap the bandages that were around his leg. He'd been injured fighting for King and country, as the Napoleonic wars raged on. Now it was Deborah's responsibility to do everything she could to restore him – and the other men here – back to full health.

"This wound looks a good deal better today," she murmured to herself, not put off by the sight of the raw skin beneath. "Another poultice, I think, to ensure there's no infection, and then we'll wrap it up again." She smiled at Mr. Griggs as he nodded, his expression set hard against the pain. "You'll soon be on your way home again, Mr. Griggs."

The man nodded, although his face was now a little pale. "That's good," he said, quietly. "Although I'll miss you, Deborah."

She shook her head at him, a chuckle escaping from her. "You'll find someone to give your heart to soon enough, Mr. Griggs," she replied, folding up the bandage so that they might be washed and then reused. "My heart is here."

WALKING BACK through the chapel in order to find all that she would need to dress Mr. Grigg's leg, Deborah reflected for a moment on what her life had become. As an orphan, she had been brought up by the nuns in this place, right in the middle of London. The nuns had given her everything she required, including an education and ensuring that she spoke and acted in an appropriate manner. One of the nuns had been a lady of quality who had turned her back on the wealth and the grandness of her life and had come to the abbey to serve and give of herself out of love for God. It was she who had educated Deborah and as a result, Deborah spoke well and always acted with decorum.

Having had such a blessed start to her life, it seemed almost natural that she should want to become a nun just as soon as she was able. She had no other experience of life other than living in the abbey. Mother Superior, however, was not quite certain that this was the right time for Deborah to take her orders, for whatever reason. As much as that frustrated Deborah, she had no other choice but to accept that she would have to wait for a time for, as Mother Superior had often reminded her, God's timing was always perfect.

Humming softly to herself, Deborah soon found what she needed and began to prepare the poultice for Mr. Griggs. This had been her work for some time now, ever since injured men had been sent back from the war with no-one to help take care of them. The abbey had been opened up almost at once and she had lost herself in the daily – and sometimes nightly – task of caring for the sick and the injured. The other nuns were vigilant in both their prayers and their care of the men, knowing that it was their duty to do so. Deborah did as much as she could, finding that the men were eager for both physical care and spiritual assistance. Oft times, she would be asked to pray for them, which she did without question. She shared many a conversation with the injured men and had begun to consider those who had been here the longest as her dear friends. Mr. Griggs, for example, would soon be on his way home once his leg had completely healed and he was able to walk again. For the moment, she enjoyed their conversations and their laughter, even though he was remarkably persistent in his wish to marry her!

Deborah laughed to herself and shook her head as she began to mix the poultice together. It was not the first time she had been asked for her hand in marriage and, most likely, it would not be the last. But marriage had never been something Deborah wanted to pursue. A nun did not marry. A nun did not have dreams of such things, and so, therefore, she had closed her mind entirely to the idea. She would take her vows soon enough, whenever Mother Superior felt it was the right time, and her life would continue on here as it had always done.

"Did you hear the news?"

Deborah turned her head to see one of the other nuns, Martha, hurrying towards her, her face bright with what appeared to be relief.

"Martha," she murmured, turning towards her. "What news? Is something wrong?"

"The war," Martha said, excitedly. "It seems the war is coming to an end!"

Deborah's eyes widened, her heart quickening in her chest. "Napoleon has been defeated?"

Martha smiled. "It seems that he soon will be," she said, closing her eyes with relief for a moment. "There is a fresh hope that he will be defeated entirely within the next few days. Oh, we must continue to pray for peace!"

Deborah nodded fervently. "Yes, of course," she agreed, quickly. "I will. I will do that this very afternoon, once I have finished in the abbey."

Martha pressed Deborah's arm. "You do such good work here, Deborah," she smiled. "God will bless you for it." She let go of Deborah's arm and walked back towards the chapel, ready to help with the injured men. Deborah followed her with her eyes for a moment or two, her mind filled with thoughts of what life here would be like when the war came to an end. The chapel would be empty of men. There would be no beds or mats strewn across it, no cries for help or of pain. She would no longer have the same duty to care for the sick and the injured as she did at this present moment. Of course, there was plenty that needed to be done outside the abbey walls, for London was stricken with desperate poverty. Deborah knew they could find some way to help these people.

"I must pray for peace," Deborah murmured to herself, turning back to pick up the poultice and some fresh bandages before following after Martha to go back into the chapel. She would see to Mr. Griggs and then return to her rooms to pray.

It did not quite work out as Deborah had intended. After seeing to Mr. Griggs, Mr. Hunter had complained of being terribly thirsty and so Deborah had fetched him something to drink, only to see that the wound to his side was oozing through the bandages. That had needed careful attention and she had been forced to stitch the wound closed. It was not the first time she had needed to do so, having become quite adept at closing wounds, but Mr. Hunter had grunted and groaned with every second of her stitching. It had taken longer than she had thought and, by the time she had finished, Mr. Hunter was grey-faced and sweating. She had needed to give him some laudanum in order to help him rest, to lose himself in a dreamless slumber away from the pain that was obviously lacing through him. One he had fallen into a restful sleep, she had made to walk back to her quarters, only for bread and soup to be brought in for the men. She had helped serve that and had needed to feed some of the weakest men, encouraging them to eat as much as they could. It was always difficult to see men in such pain and harder still to see some fade away until they took their last breath. Deborah tried not to allow her mind to settle on such things, however, recalling instead the many, many men who had recovered and had left the abbey, returning to their home and their families that they had left behind.

Her body was tired. Her legs were aching and still, Deborah knew that there was no time for resting. She needed to pray, needed to ask God to bring about the peace that would be such a blessing to the country. She wanted an end to the fighting, an end to the injured men that seemed to constantly stream into London. She wanted peace and restoration for the countries involved. Determined that she would pray as she had intended, Deborah made her way slowly up the long flight of stone stairs towards her room, which was both small and yet very personal. It had nothing of particular interest within, other than a small bed and small chest of drawers for her clothes, for she had been taught that things such as jewelry or the like were mere fripperies. They were adornments which she did not need, not if she was intending to take her orders. Deborah had never questioned her way of living since it was all she had ever known. Yes, her day to day life could be difficult and yes, she was often weary to the bone, but she knew that her work and her dedication came from a love for God, just as it did for the other nuns. She was happy here, all in all, although she wished she could tell what it was that held Mother Superior back from allowing her to take her orders.

"Deborah?"

She turned around with a smile, seeing Mother Superior standing at the bottom of the steps, her lined face holding the usual quiet expression that was so familiar to Deborah.

"Yes, Mother?"

"Might you come with me for a moment?" Mother Superior asked, gesturing towards her own small rooms. "I have something I need to speak to you about."

Deborah nodded and turned around at once, her tiredness suddenly forgotten as a fresh hope began to beat in her chest. Was this to be the start of her life as a nun? Was Mother Superior about to tell her that she would be able to take her orders soon?

Her footsteps quickened on the staircase as she hurried down towards Mother Superior's rooms. Mother Superior had a small room, in addition to her bedroom, that was used for letter writing and meetings. Private conversations took place within, correspondence was sent to her there and, on occasion, those wishing to become a nun were sent here to be questioned by Mother Superior. Mother Superior, whilst always kind and gentle in how she spoke, always spoke with a certainty and a sureness that told Deborah that there was never any possibility of questioning the authority that had been given to her. Deborah had to continually trust that Mother Superior knew what was best for Deborah and had, therefore, simply needed to accept that she would not be taking her holy orders any time soon.

"Although," she murmured aloud, walking towards the small room where Mother Superior had just entered, "that might all be about to change."

A knot of excitement settled in her stomach as she walked inside, feeling the sense of peace settle over her as she sat down. This room always felt so tranquil, which must be a reflection of Mother Superior herself. She waited patiently as Mother Superior sat down at the small, wooden desk, noticing the piece of paper that sat in front of her.

"Deborah," Mother Superior began, clasping her hands in front of her. "We have heard the news that the war is soon to be at an end."

"Yes, yes, I know," Deborah replied, eagerly. "Martha said as much to me. I was just about to go to my rooms and pray that it would occur soon."

Mother Superior nodded, a gentle smile on her face. "Your work here has been tireless," she said, quietly. "I have seen the way you care for those injured men. You have been the light and the hope that they have needed, Deborah. You have cared for both their injuries and for their souls." Her smile faded. "I have watched you hold the hand of a dying man and stay with him until his body is all that remains of him. You have prayed for them, watched over them, cared for them and given as much of yourself as you could for them."

Deborah, unused to hearing such praise from Mother Superior, did not quite know what to do. Looking down at her hands, she closed her eyes and reminded herself not to become proud of what was being said. Silently, she prayed and thanked God that He had given her the desire to care for the sick and the injured, prayed that she would not grow weary of her work.

"I have had a letter this morning," Mother Superior continued, as Deborah looked up at her. "I think, Deborah, that this is something that you need to do."

"Do?" Deborah repeated, a slight frown forming between her brows. "What is it that I must do, Mother Superior?"

Mother Superior picked up the letter, read it again, sighed and set it back down on the desk between them. Deborah felt her fingers itch to reach across and pick it up so that she might read it for herself but wisely chose to fight the urge to do so.

"There is a gentleman," Mother Superior began, her voice soft. "He has been terribly injured and requires care."

"A gentleman," Deborah repeated, her frown growing steadily. "That is unusual for him to request aid from the convent, is it not?"

Mother Superior nodded, although a slight twinkle caught her sharp blue eyes. "It is not the gentleman himself who has requested that someone here go to attend him," she said, by way of explanation. "It is Lady Markham."

"His wife?"

Mother Superior shook her head. "His sister," she said, quietly. "Lord Abernathy is a Duke and insisted on going to war despite his title. He was injured, as I have said, losing a couple of fingers from one hand and his face badly disfigured on one side. But it is not simply his wounds that need tending, Deborah. Lady Markham writes that she barely knows her brother any longer and feels as though he is being pulled in by darkness. She requests our aid in pulling him from this malevolence."

Deborah nodded, feeling her heart thumping furiously in her chest. She knew why Mother Superior was speaking to her of this, realizing that the lady thought that *she* would be best suited to leaving the abbey and going to live with Lord Abernathy's staff for a time. However, the very idea of leaving the only home she'd ever really known and going somewhere entirely new frightened her terribly.

"Deborah," Mother Superior continued, as though she could see into Deborah's heart. "I know that this can be quite intimidating for someone who has never really lived away from the abbey, but I have the feeling that this is meant to be your path. After all, you have been very well educated and know how you are to speak to someone like the Duke. You will manage very well there, I am sure. Once you return, you can take your orders."

Deborah licked her lips, not quite sure how to respond.

"You have such a brightness in your heart that it

cannot fail to touch Lord Abernathy's darkness," Mother Superior finished, leaning towards Deborah a little. "I can see that within you, Deborah, even if you can not. Lord Abernathy needs someone such as you to help him see the joy of life again, to remove the dark shades of the past from his eyes. You can do that, Deborah. You can give him the hope he needs to see life for what it is." She sat back in her chair, her expression serious. "Although I will not pretend to you that it will be easy, nor that he will be glad of your presence. It may take a good deal of time for him to accept you within the house and only then will you be able to do what you can to help him."

This did not sound like a particularly desirous situation and Deborah felt herself rebelling against it almost at once. A Duke, who had more money, wealth and influence than any other person in England, aside from the King, would not exactly be pleased to have a nun within his own house, especially if he was not expecting her! What would happen if he instructed her to leave? Was she to remain regardless, knowing that Lady Markham, his sister, had requested her to stay? Or would she have to do as the Duke asked and quit the house?

"I can tell that you have a good many thoughts on the matter," Mother Superior said, softly, drawing Deborah's attention. "I will not force you in this, Deborah. This is something I feel is being set out for *you* to do, but you must not allow yourself to be overwhelmed by it. Pray about it. Consider it. And then return to me with your answer."

Nodding slowly, Deborah pushed herself out of her chair. "But I cannot take my orders until I return?" she asked, feeling herself rebelling against the idea. "You will not allow me to take them unless I go?"

Mother Superior looked surprised and Deborah immediately felt a flare of guilt in her chest, although she did not take back what she had said.

"I will pray about the matter," Mother Superior replied, eventually. "I shall give the matter much thought and will allow you time to do the same." Her expression softened, her eyes filled with understanding. "I know that you are eager to take your vows, Deborah, but I must know for certain that this is where you belong."

A little hurt, Deborah lowered her head. "I did not think that I had ever given you reason to doubt me," she replied.

Mother Superior walked around the desk and came towards Deborah, one hand resting lightly on her arm. "No, it has never been a question of that," she said, encouragingly. "Think of it as a question in my own mind. A question that I have not yet been able to answer. I believe that there may be something different for you, Deborah, than what you yourself have planned." She let go of Deborah's arm. "But I will not prevent you from remaining here instead of going to Lord Abernathy's if that is what you feel led to do. And, of course, your orders will always be on my mind. I will keep praying about the matter until an answer comes to me with clarity."

Deborah let out a long breath, feeling as though she already knew the answer to the question as to whether or not she would leave the abbey. She wanted to pray about it, wanted to come to the conclusion that she was required here, but the weight of the letter and the desperation of Lady Markham had already begun to settle on her soul.

"When must I leave?" she asked, a little dully. "And for how long?"

Mother Superior smiled softly, as though she had been expecting this answer. "Tomorrow," she said, gently. "And Lady Markham has requested that you remain for one month initially, no matter what the Duke himself says." She smiled as Deborah nodded, obviously seeing the frustration and flickering uncertainty in Deborah's eyes. "You have nothing to fear, Deborah. The Duke will not harm you, for he is not that sort of gentleman. He is a man lost in pain, lost in torment. Help him find his way back to the light, back to the hope and the joy that he once had and I am certain that he will be grateful for it."

"I must hope so," Deborah replied, her stomach twisting painfully as she walked away from Mother Superior and back towards the door. "I shall go and prepare myself for tomorrow's departure, then."

"Thank you, Deborah," Mother Superior murmured, as Deborah pulled the door open. "I truly believe that this is the path you are meant to take. Do not shirk from it. Who knows what will come of your presence in Lord Abernathy's home?"

Deborah could not find anything to say, nodding towards Mother Superior before closing the door and walking back towards the staircase and her own rooms. Deep within her, she felt a trembling take a hold of her, her heart beating so furiously that she became a little nauseous. To leave the abbey was one thing, but to go to the home of an injured gentleman who did not even want her to be in his house was quite another! What would she say if he demanded that she leave him? What would she do? Mother Superior might be convinced that this was what Deborah was meant to do but she herself felt no such certainty.

Settling her nerves with a sheer force of will, Deborah climbed the steps and hurried towards her own little room. The familiarity of it comforted Deborah's heart, reminding her that she would be gone for only a month. She would return to this place after only a few weeks, glad to come back to the one place she thought of as home.

Besides, Lord Abernathy could not be too difficult now, could he?

CHAPTER TWO

Harksbury Hall was a day's travel away from London. Deborah had risen earlier than usual when the sky was still dark and the sun not even a thought in the sky. She had gone to pray for a good hour or so, having been so lost in anxiety that she had felt as though a cloud surrounded her, darkening her vision and rendering her almost useless.

The coach that was taking her to Lord Abernathy's home was dark and cold, the chill wind seeming to come in every nook and cranny. Deborah had tried to sleep as it had rattled out of London, but her fears had been unwilling to let her rest, forcing her eyes open and her mind to tumble with thoughts. What would Lord Abernathy be like? Was his injury truly as serious as Mother Superior had said? Over and over, she came up with visions of what he might look like, wondering what it was that had hurt his face so terribly.

War was truly horrible. It took lives whenever it pleased, pulling life from both the poor and the rich without question. She hated the evilness of it, the cruelty that left such an ugly mark. Silently, she prayed for peace yet again, praying that the injured soldiers seeking aid would soon come to a stop. She prayed that the men would one day all be restored to their families, that those who had lost a husband or a father, brother or a son, would be comforted in their grief.

And then she prayed for herself. She prayed for strength and courage for what was to come, worrying that she wouldn't be given a warm welcome by the Duke. Her hands twisted in her lap as she looked outside, seeing nothing but countryside for miles beyond. Just how far away was Harksbury Hall?

A sudden jerk had Deborah's eyes flying open, her heart slamming into her chest as she looked all about her. They had arrived at the Duke's residence, it seemed, as she was entirely unprepared. Only just realizing that she had fallen asleep, Deborah rubbed at her eyes frantically, praying that she did not appear too disheveled.

"The servant's entrance, Miss Harland, if you please."

Deborah scrambled out of the coach as best as she could, seeing the two footmen waiting for her to accompany them. One of them had her single, small bag which he carried in for her. Deborah lifted her chin, checked that her bonnet ribbons were tied tightly and that her hair was not tumbling over her forehead and followed after them.

Harksbury Hall was one of the grandest, most imposing structures, that Deborah had ever laid eyes on. Even looking upward, she could not quite see the top. In the cold greyness of the day, the sun did not sparkle on the seemingly hundreds of windows, although that did not detract from the impressiveness of the house.

Quietly, Deborah wondered if Lord Abernathy was somewhere within, looking down at her and scrutinizing her carefully. A cold shiver ran down her spine and she turned her attention back towards the footmen, seeing one enter into a large red wooden door. The other waited for her to catch up and, hurrying, she stepped inside and immediately felt a rush of warmth hit her.

The kitchens were just to her left, with other rooms to her right. The servant's staircase was directly in front of her.

"She's here, Mr. Morris," one of the footmen said, dropping Deborah's bag at her feet. "That nun that Lady Markham said she'd fetch for his lordship."

Deborah opened her mouth to say that she had not taken her vows yet, only for a large, broad-shouldered older man to fix her with a stern gaze, rendering her speechless as he came towards her.

"You are not a nun," he said, frowning, his gaze running over her and sending a wave of heat up Deborah's spine. "Lady Markham was most specific."

"I – I have not yet taken my orders," Deborah stammered, feeling intimidated by the butler's presence. "But I will do so very soon. Here." She dug about for a moment, before pulling out a small note from her bag. "Mother Superior has written a note to reassure you of my abilities."

The frown did not leave Mr. Morris' face but he took the letter from her, broke it open and began to read. As

Deborah watched, she saw the frustration leave Mr. Morris' expression which was quickly replaced with a look of relief.

"Very good," he muttered, folding up the note and putting it in his pocket. "I am sorry, Miss Harland, but I was expecting someone in a habit. You understand, of course."

"Of course," she repeated, awash with relief. "And am I to meet Lord Abernathy?"

The butler hesitated, his grey eyes darting from place to place. "I think," he said, slowly, "that you might want to put your things away first. We have a room for you, of course, but it is above stairs." He smiled tightly. "You are to have the governess's rooms, although they have not been used in some time. They have been aired and prepared for your arrival."

Deborah smiled, feeling a little more at ease. "I thank you," she said, inclining her head. "That is very kind of you."

The butler nodded, although the air of tension had not quite dissipated. "I think I should be honest with you, Miss Harland. Lord Abernathy is not aware that you have been sent for and will not display any sort of gratitude at your arrival."

Deborah nodded. "Yes, I am aware of that."

"Oh?" The butler looked surprised.

"Lady Markham's letter made that quite clear," Deborah explained, seeing the look of relief etch itself into the older man's expression. "I will not be afraid of such a demeanor, Mr. Morris. I am quite prepared for it." She tried to put as much determination into her voice as she could, even though her heart was still beating rather quickly in her chest. "You have no need to concern yourself for my sake."

Mr. Morris nodded, tipped his head and considered her for a few moments. "Very well," he said, eventually. "I shall have your things sent up to your rooms and once you have met Lord Abernathy, I will have the housekeeper, Mrs. Denton, show you to your rooms. You will have your meals brought up to you, of course, but you are always welcome below stairs and to seek myself or Mrs. Denton out, should you have any questions or concerns."

"Thank you," Deborah replied, relieved that she was to have at least one member of staff within the household that she could rely on for help. "Might you tell me more about Lord Abernathy's condition?"

Mr. Morris grimaced but gestured for her to begin to climb the stairs. He followed after, talking as they went.

"Lord Abernathy is, of course, the Duke and therefore would not have been expected to fight," he said, as Deborah hurried up the staircase. "He has a younger brother, however, and so decided that he wished to do just that, stating that his brother could easily take over the title and continue the family line if something were to happen to him."

Deborah's eyes widened. "Goodness," she murmured, as they walked into the long, bright hallway. "That is a little unusual, is it not?"

Mr. Morris nodded. "Very much so. Lady Markham was most distressed but His Grace was not at all inclined to listen to her. Therefore, he went to fight and the next thing we hear is that he has been injured and will require considerable care."

Deborah looked all about her, taking in the grandeur of the house, aware of just how small it made her feel. "I see."

"His hand has lost two fingers," the butler continued. "And his face, on one side, has been badly injured. There are the usual poultices and bandages in place but His Grace is not at all eager to have himself bound up in such a way. It is only because of his sister's insistence that he allows himself to be looked after at all."

Deborah frowned. "He does not want to recover?"

The butler hesitated, then shook his head. "I am not quite certain what it is that His Grace struggles with," he replied, carefully, "But he is not a man who gives any appearance of wishing to get better and return to his former life. Instead, he cries out about the war, states that he would have been better off in the grave than returned to his life here in such a state of brokenness." He sighed and Deborah felt her heart sink to the floor. "His Grace is not the man he once was," the butler finished, honestly. "I will be honest with you, Miss Harland, and tell you that I am struggling terribly with his demeanor, for I do not know what to do."

Swallowing her concern, Deborah fixed a smile to her lips. "That is more than understandable," she said, trying to find some sort of encouragement for him. "I have seen and cared for many injured soldiers, and some of them have been in the very depths of despondency for some days. It is only when they begin to recover that a fresh light seems to return to their soul."

"Then I pray that you will be able to bring such a light back to Lord Abernathy," the butler replied, fervently. "His sister, Lady Markham, is due to reside with us for a time by the end of the week. I know that she will be most grateful to you for anything you have been able to do."

They walked up yet another flight of stairs – although this one was much grander than the servant's staircase.

Deborah found herself astonished with the opulence that surrounded her. Having been brought up in the abbey where any such ornaments or trinkets were discouraged, it was almost overwhelming to see so many things littering almost every surface. The Duke was, of course, exceedingly wealthy.

Ahead of them, a door opened and, her attention caught, Deborah saw a woman step out of the door, pulling it closed softly behind her.

"Ah, Mrs. Denton," Mr. Morris said, with a small smile. "May I introduce you to Miss Harland? She has been sent from the abbey."

"I have not yet taken my orders," Deborah said, by way of explanation as Mrs. Denton gave her a confused look. "But Mother Superior has sent me in the hope that I might be of some aid to Lord Abernathy."

Mrs. Denton, who had grey hair pinned back into a tight bun, a thin, pinched face and the biggest brown eyes Deborah had ever seen, shook her head. Her slim frame seemed to be tight with tension. The paleness in her face warned Deborah that all was not well with the lady.

"I am glad to meet you, of course, Miss Harland," Mrs. Denton said, quickly, "But I cannot suggest that you meet His Grace at this present time. He is.....not in the happiest of moods."

Deborah held Mrs. Denton's gaze, seeing two spots of color appear in the older lady's cheeks. Was she embarrassed to have to speak so openly about her master? Or had she been humiliated in some way by Lord Abernathy's words, her embarrassment due to his harshness?

"I have come to see Lord Abernathy, have I not?" Deborah asked, softly, trying to push away the fear coiling within her. "I must be able to help him in some way, and I cannot do that unless I meet with him."

"He does not know of your presence here," Mrs. Denton replied, urgently, as though this was the only reason required to set Deborah away from Lord Abernathy. "He will be frustrated with his sister for doing such a thing and given how he is this afternoon, I cannot think that adding to his woes will be wise for either of you."

Deborah tried to smile, refusing to listen to the warning in her mind. "I will simply introduce myself, that is all," she said, even though her heart was pounding with fright. "If he throws me from the room and demands that I leave the house, I have no intention of turning tail and running from the estate. Lady Markham was quite clear in her letter that I was to remain for at least a month. I have every intention of doing so, for I want to be able to help Lord Abernathy as best I can."

Mrs. Denton hesitated, sharing a look with Mr. Morris that Deborah could not quite make out.

"I do think it would be best if you waited for Lady Markham's visit," Mr. Morris said, eventually. "But if you are quite certain, then, Mrs. Denton, I think we may attempt to introduce Miss Harland together."

Mrs. Denton sighed heavily. "He is in a sour mood, Mr. Morris."

"When is he not?" Mr. Morris replied, sharply, surprising Deborah with his tone. "Besides, it may be best for Miss Harland to see the Duke as he really is. We have no need to hide the truth from her now, do we?"

"I would protect you if I could, Miss Harland," Mrs. Denton replied, one hand now on the door handle. "You do look very young and quite timid, if I may say so."

Deborah allowed herself a small smile. "I am but one and twenty, Mrs. Denton," she replied, "but I have quite significant experience when it comes to injured men. I have seen a good deal of strife and trouble, and I do hope that God has sent me here for the sole purpose of using that experience to aid Lord Abernathy."

Her words seemed to encourage Mrs. Denton a little for the lady sighed, nodded and then opened the door wide.

It was time to meet Lord Abernathy.

WHAT WILL Deborah do when she meets Lord Abernathy? Click here to get the rest of the story on the Kindle Store! The Duke's Saving Grace

JOIN MY MAILING LIST

Sign up for my newsletter to stay up to date on new releases, contests, giveaways, freebies, and deals!

Free book with signup!

Monthly Facebook Giveaways! Books and Amazon gift cards!
Join me on Facebook: https://www. facebook.com/rosepearsonauthor

Website: www.RosePearsonAuthor.com

Follow me on Goodreads: Author Page

You can also follow me on Bookbub!
Click on the picture below – see the Follow button?

Printed in Poland
by Amazon Fulfillment
Poland Sp. z o.o., Wrocław